THE HAPPIEST PLACE IN SPACE!

A CRUISE BROTHERS NOVEL

RON COLLINS

JEFF COLLINS

SKYFOX PUBLISHING
Science Fiction

The Happiest Place in Space!
A Cruise Brothers Novel
Copyright © 2024 by Ron Collins & Jeff Colins
All rights reserved.

Songs:
"Frisky" © Jeff Collins & Ron Collins
"Happy Family Fun" © Jeff Collins
"Small Universe After All" © Jeff Collins

Cover Design by Ron Collins
Image: yogysic

This book is licensed for your personal enjoyment only. All rights reserved. This is a work of fiction. All incidents, dialog, and characters are products of the authors' imagination. Any resemblance to persons living or dead is purely coincidental. This book, or parts thereof, may not be reproduced in any form without permission.

Skyfox Publishing

ISBN-10: 1-946176-52-4
ISBN-13: 078-1-946176-52-3

For Karen and Lisa

The Cruise Sisters in Law!

CHAPTER 1

The cherry-cheeked entertainment director took a pull on his opalescent jumpdust dispenser, breathed it deeply into his lungs, then exhaled a cloud of glittering particles into the stolid air of the now empty, but otherwise expansive star lounge. The sound of cleaners cleaning made a din in the background. An assistant brought the director another drink.

Falling to the floor, the particles scintillated.

Dude was a beefy guy, which made a certain kind of sense because Dude spent half his life out where a hundred extra kilos doesn't hurt at all—*and* he has infinite access to star cruise food.

With a cruise director's salary and nothing left to do, what the hell do you expect?

Shoving the dispenser behind his ear, the entertainment director shuffled his weight around in the chair, then looked up.

"Next?" he called out in a voice raw enough to say he'd been doing the jumpdust for a long time.

From side stage, Lyn Moore, the smarter, better-looking half of the Moore Brothers, scratched the back of his head with one hand, the other hooking his guitar by the neck. "What the hell?" he said.

James, the *other* smarter, better-looking half of the duo, peered out, too, looping his instrument to settle over his shoulder as he scanned the director. He felt a little silly wearing the vivid blue and yellow duds Lyn had been so on and on about *(it'll go great with the stage! You'll see!)*. While Lyn had probably been right on the aesthetics, James still thought the long bell-bottom pants and fluffy sleeved shirt made him feel like something out of *Glam-Bam*, the intergalactic trade journal that was always trying to find new ways to make a splash. All they needed now was a prismatic laser ball and they'd fit right into TekniFab Crew Six, the group that was on the front edge of this week's standard issue.

Sellouts.

The director's expression didn't give James any comfort.

"Dude doesn't seem happy to see us, does he?"

"Maybe not," Lyn replied, "but look at those girls!"

"They aren't all women," James said.

"All the ones *I* care about are."

James rolled his eyes. This was a Galactic Cruise Lines ship. The hosts—human and alien, men, women, and everything between—were going to be strictly off-limits, no matter how stunning they looked dressed up in their catsuits, princess spandex, and star power dresses.

He wondered if any of them were holographic.

The place was closed until launch, so they were probably all real.

Still.

"Focus, Lyn."

"Oh, believe me, I'm focused."

Feeling a lost cause, James studied the entertainment director.

Dude most definitely did not appear happy to see anyone, better yet another in the long line of acts he'd been dealing with all day. Actually, Dude's several hundred pounds of mass appeared to be sweating under the load of full gravity that was mandated at the docking station. Dude had less hair on top, more on the sides, and a dome of a head that glistened with the glow of jumpdust residue. His cheeks puffed out as red as the holo cartoons of the gnomes and dwarves the Galactic Cruise Line advertised so profoundly.

"The Happiest Place in Space!" James muttered, then sighed. "I never thought we'd be auditioning for a goddamned cruise line."

"I know!" Lyn said. "I told you things would work out."

James tried not to laugh.

Based on the packed corridor outside the audition hall when they first arrived, Entertainment Director Dude's patience was probably as thin as the pitiful seat of his poor little pants right about now. He looked half frazzled with the audition process and *fully* zoned for the Most Happy Happy Hour in the Galaxy ™, which, since the audition was being held at the cruiser's Star Cabaret, the hosts and server bots were already in the process of setting up.

The platform behind the director buzzed with activity.

The three girls Lyn was so fixated on were working, as were an entire royal phalanx of motorized doodads and sweeper bots.

Glasses clinked and self-driving buffer machines whined as they disinfected the floor.

"Next!" the cruise director coughed again.

"Asshole," Lyn said. "That dust stick poking out of his round head makes him look like a pasty-skinned slogger slug with a pencil-thin hard-on. Let's show him what real music sounds like."

With a pump of his fist, Lyn strode to center stage.

"Rock and roll, baby!"

James hustled behind, holding the neck of his guitar to keep it from flapping off the strap—which he immediately thought would be a great title for another Moore Brothers song.

Where you at boy, my daddy say the other day,
nowhere Pa, I had my say,
cause I saw the trap, trap, trap,
couldn't tell him we were just out
flap, flap, flapping off the strap!

The melody was forming as he caught up to his brother at center stage.

Three scintillating microphone bots floated around on systems set to full antigravity, and the AI synthesizer they'd tone-mapped to earlier took their place behind them.

James hoped the thing would work out all right.

Bringing new talent into the mix was always touchy, but you do what you have to.

Lyn, of course, had struck up an immediate friendship with the thing.

"All right," the entertainment director said. "Who are you, and why do I care?"

Lyn whipped his guitar around and took a Massive Rock Star pose that came complete with a snarl.

Crap. Here we go again.

"We're the M—" Lyn started before James cut him off.

"We're the Cruise Brothers," James said rapidly, understanding fully well that the word Lyn had been planning to end his introduction with would have included a reference to their mother and ended in something that rhymed with the phrase "Space Muckers."

They needed this job too much for Lyn to pull that kind of crap.

Lyn blinked wide eyes back at James, and—luckily—seemed to cool down a bit.

"Uh … yeah," Lyn said, relaxing a touch and adding a cheesy grin. "We're … we're the *Star* Cruise Brothers."

James rolled his eyes. *Always with the one-upmanship, eh, bro?*

Can't be letting you have all the fun now, can I? Lyn's slanted smile shot back.

"Cute," the director said. "I hope you're not a comedy act."

"No, sir," James said. "We're musicians."

"Oh, joy."

The director pulled the jumpdust stick from behind his ear, took another hit, then peered more closely at them.

"Are you two clones?" the director said. "Because, you know, we're not that kind of cruise."

"Twins, sir," James said.

"Identical," Lyn added.

"You don't farkin say."

"Brothers from the same mother-er-er-er-er!" Lyn sang. "Hey, that would make a great song."

"Please be quiet," James muttered under his breath, glancing at Lyn mostly to shut him up.

The clean-cut Galactic Cruise lines may not do clones, but rumors said they weren't above catering to the darker sides of the collective capitalism of the outer ring while they pedaled their wholesome fun, fun, fun attitude to the families they carted around the galaxy. If there was anything true in his life it was that he'd learned to not trust Lyn to say the right thing at the wrong time. Or the right thing at any time, for that matter.

"Don't mind my brother," James said. "We can give you our mother's nexus node if you're interested in her story of the day we were born. I'm sure she'd love to chat with a real live entertainment director."

The director recoiled. "Oh, hell, no."

"All right, then. We're very happy to be here, auditioning for the Happiest Place in Space, aren't we, Lyn?" He gave his brother the slant eye.

Lyn kept his yap shut and gave an exaggerated nod in the affirmative.

Which was good.

After the trick Lyn pulled with the band last week, it was good to see he was having a day where he was almost able to stay between the lines.

"Great," the director said, chuckling. "Enough with the flabberjabbing. Let's see what you got."

"Excellent," James said.

"Rock and roll!" Lyn added.

Both boys took guitars in hand.

"We call this one, 'Happy Family Fun,'" Lyn said. "We wrote it earlier today just for all the great people here on the *Galactic Epic*!"

He ripped in with a big chord, AI drums kicked it, and their voices merged into that blood-tone magic that formed whenever they played together.

Happy family fun
Happy family fun
Happy family fun for the whole family fun

Taking the kids on a fantastic journey
Shootin' stars right out of the sky
So much mischief better bring the attorney
Spare no expense, don't ask why

The director's shiny head bounced up and down in rhythm with the song. His hand tapped a snappy line.

Taking the kids on a wonderful voyage
Get away from the rut on the earth
No crappy jobs or homework to forage
Just acned teens in character suits

Happy family fun
Happy family fun
Happy family fun for the whole family fun

Lyn nodded at James, which James knew was a sign for *"do you see what I see from the director,"* then took another Monster Rock Star pose while slipping in a quick improvised lead.

That was the thing about the two of them—despite their differences, James couldn't deny there was a connection that happened whenever they played. Lyn may well have improvised that run on the spot, but James had known it was coming even before Lyn took the pose. He stepped back to make space.

A getaway in time and space

THE HAPPIEST PLACE IN SPACE!

A new adventure, take our picture please
I look around not a familiar face
No one here knows what Uncle Johnny did
All the stands with family friendly fare
Hide the scars from all the childhood trauma
Spend $50 on an over-stuffed bear
No one here knows what Father Rusty did

The director actually laughed at that stanza, though his expression seemed hard to judge. Screw it, James thought. Time to have some fun.

Then he ripped into his own solo, and Lynn stepped in behind *him* this time. They were good, he thought. If they could just be on stage all the time, everything would be pulsar spray and nova dust. It was all the rest of the stuff that was problematic.

Hey, there's the mouse!
There's the prince!
There's the princess too!

Me and wifey on a relaxing cruise ship
But hard to romance with kids on their phone
Here's some money for games and cheese sticks
At 10 years old they'll be fine on their own

Happy family fun
Happy family fun
Happy family fun for the whole family fun

A few of the hosts had stopped their cleaning and preparing now, listening rather than doing their work.

Attention was good, right?

Lyn grabbed a floating mic, let his guitar swing free, and took front stage as the rhythm took a staccato march beat.

Fellow passengers, welcome to the Epic! Are you ready to Limboooo!!!
Potato sack race is today at 4 pm
And tonight, after you put the kids to bed, the Mr. Epic contest is starting at 9 pm!!
All the hot guys will be gyrating in your face to win your vote as the most handsome hunk on the ship.

Hey, there's the mouse!
There's the prince!
There's the princess too!

A s their guitars faded, several of the servers applauded.

"I liked that," the director said. "Very catchy."

"Thank you," James said.

"We have to do something about that middle bit. Funny as hell, but no one comes to the Galactic Cruise lines for that kind of trauma. And, really, what's up with the mouse thing?"

"It's not a problem," James said.

"What?" Lyn added too quickly. "You want to cut the lyrics?"

James blanched.

So close.

They'd been so very close.

The director nodded. "Of course, I do." The rough part of his voice was back.

"No can do, Sherlock," Lyn said.

"Pardon me?"

"We're not some kind of quasar quacks who just showed up in the airlock on a lark. We're artists! We've been signed before and everything. And now *you* come along and try to tell *us* we have to cut our work? Who do you think you are?"

"Never mind," the director said, waving dismissively. "I don't need that kind of crap on my ship. Just go on and get out of here."

"What?"

The man sucked hard on his jumpdust pipe and waved them off stage from amid a glittering cloud.

"Next!" he said.

CHAPTER 2

With their guitars hanging from their shoulders like gleaming backpacks, Lyn and James tumbled off the stage and into a stairway down—pinballing their way through the few waiting acts that remained, including a dance trio from Zaxadar and a pair of grape-skinned, five-armed jugglers of a species James had never seen.

Their footsteps echoed off naked gunmetal walls.

The corridor was cold, the décor battleship gray.

No expenses spared on heating the help.

"I can't believe you did that!" James said.

"Did what?" Lyn replied. "You mean stand up for our creative integrity?"

"The man gave us a compliment!"

"Backhanded as you can get! And what about you up there? Calling us the Cruise Brothers? Can you get any more lame?"

"Better than the Middly Piddly."

"The Middly Piddly would have been farkin'

famous if you'd just let us play the Crush-Rock like I said we should."

James gritted his teeth. "I can't believe I let you get us up there in these disastrous pajama costumes, better yet put your big foot into your bigger mouth—just as we were closing a deal!"

"Well, at least my foot damned well fits."

James pulled up.

"Come again? What the hell does that mean?"

Lyn paused three steps later. "It means just what I said it means."

"At least my foot fits?"

"Yeah. Duh."

"Screw it," James said.

They clopped down the final stair and into the corridor that led to the airlocks and off the ship.

As they made the exit foyer, a thin voice came from behind.

"Excuse me?"

They turned to find an ambassador robot hovering in mid-air, a standard pyramidal object about as big as a person's head with multiple lights that flashed at each of its four points.

"What the hell?" Lyn said.

"Antigrav," James replied.

"I know what antigravity is, you dolt. Why is this thing here to begin with?"

"The entertainment director would like to offer you a position," the bot said in a soft, but purposefully mechanical voice.

"Ah," Lyn said, stepping forward, and pulling his

billowing shirt back into place. "I knew the bastard would come around eventually. That makes sense now, doesn't it? We're obviously too good to let go on a lark like that."

Lights flashed on the pyramid.

"What are the terms?"

The ambassador bot rolled its colors from red and purple to orange and pink. "Terms are standard scale."

"We want a raise!" Lyn called.

"I think you misunderstand," the bot replied.

"Oh, no, it is most certainly you who does not understand!" Red passion rose in Lyn's cheeks.

"The offer is not for both of you," the pyramid replied.

Lyn cocked his head, an expression of deep concern growing. "I'm sorry, I can't work without my brother."

"The offer is not for you."

Lyn, in his yellow costume, looked at James.

James, draped in silken blue, looked back.

"You only want me?" James said.

"The entertainment director needs a hall act for outside the Crab Nebula Bar and Bakery. You will suffice."

A moment of stagnation came over the corridor.

Lyn burst out laughing. "Ha! The pearl-handled jumpduster wants you to be a glorified busker! *Wee-boy*, that's funny." He slapped his thigh.

James wrapped his hand around his guitar neck but said nothing.

"You're not actually thinking about it," Lyn said.

"You might have forgotten, brother, but we need some serious cashola now."

"Not that bad we don't."

"Says the idiot who broke up a perfectly good band all by himself."

"You know it was Kanzo and Mif that screwed it up."

"No, Lyn, I don't know that."

"Then you should have stayed with them."

"Maybe I should have," James said.

He turned to the robot.

"So," he said, "just what *is* standard scale for a galactic cruise?"

The Ambassador robot gave a number, then hung there, waiting.

The airlock buzzed.

A voice recording noted a two-minute warning before the next exit process began.

"You can't be serious," Lyn said.

James looked at Lyn.

"We need the money."

CHAPTER 3

A blast of air jettisoned Lyn out of the conveyor tram and into Cygnus Grand Central Station with enough power that he almost hit the floor. He spun around as the airlock clanged with a cold clunk that reverberated throughout the terminal. Using his guitar for something that was almost balance, Lyn staggered, gathered himself, and yelled: "And don't let the door bump your ass on the way out!"

The clamor of rushing tourists swelled through the station—which was the Galactic Cruise Lines' central hub.

The place was a huge mishmash of modern design below, with a creepy Goth-like dome of a roof that disappeared into the darkness overhead. Radiation-hardened windows opened on the gleaming silver fuselage of *Galactic Epic,* the cruiser that would take this throng of cash-ripe tourists to Aldebaran, home of Universal Galaxy World, where the Happy, Happy, Fun, Fun part of the Happy, Happy, Fun, Fun tour would totally kick in.

The dark velvet background of deep space beckoned from behind the cruiser.

"Look, Mama!" said a human kid who might have been eight. "It's a star clown!"

An *Epic* Cruise admittance pass glowed from the back of one pudgy little hand, which was balled up to point at Lyn.

Lyn suddenly felt the entirety of his yellow silk stretch pants and multi-layered, billowing shirt.

"Get out of here, kid," he said, fighting the urge to hit the brat with the guitar he still held in his hand.

That would be bad.

The instrument was a Pulsar V, with a throwback novaburst body. The action was perfect. The sound was sublime. Just holding it made him want to strike the pose. When he played it, he felt like time stood still. Which is why he named it Victoria. An exotic instrument like that deserved an exotic name like Victoria.

All he needed to make his day complete would be to take a chunk out of it on this snot-nosed kid's shinbone.

"I'm sorry," the father said as he shooed the kid away. "Little Jackson doesn't know how to behave in crowds quite yet."

"There's a news flash!" Lyn called.

The moment settled then, and Lyn found himself fully alone as the chattering crowd whirled past. He clamped his hand around the instrument's neck even tighter, feeling invisible at the same time as he was exposed and vulnerable. Even the steel wall of the airlock seemed to be taunting him.

Hulking Denebians, their skins the color of rutabagas, and their acidic scent noticeable from ten paces, were the predominant pedestrians in the station, which made sense because this Cygnus Station was built to orbit their home star. Settling down, Lyn could spot maybe fifteen different species from fifteen different systems in the crowd, and even a few humans like him. A cacophony of voices echoed languages he could never catch unless he could clip on a personal processor, which he didn't have right now.

In the distance food dispensaries smelled of warm broth and sharp condiments.

"I could use a sandwich," he said.

He didn't have an account here, though—or anywhere else for that matter.

So, no sandwich.

"What an idiot," he said, shaking his head and muttering under his breath at the memory of James's face as the coppers had pushed him into the airlock.

"I can't believe James did that."

He may not know what to do with himself now, but he did know one thing: James would never cut it without him. And idiot or not, Lyn didn't want his brother to bomb. They were twins, after all, and people were stupid. A James catastrophe was bad news everywhere. And worse, replays of James playing in the corridor of the *Galactic Epic* would get out.

No one would be able to tell the difference.

Busking in the cruise line.

His own career would be scarred for life!

This is the final boarding call for the Galactic Epic, cruise to Aldebaran Universal Galaxy World, a voice echoed across the expanse. *Gates close in five minutes.*

The phrase was repeated in a language that was mostly squeaks and pops, then another.

Lyn's heart raced.

His gaze went to the *Galactic Epic*, docked outside the station.

He had to get back in there, or James was doomed.

A towering wall loomed ten stories strong between the station and the ship, seeming to go on forever. At least four elegantly configured boarding ramps connected to the gleaming silver fuselage of the *Galactic Epic*. Each with auto-transfer tubes leading to four airlock systems.

Security was tight there, though.

No chance of getting in.

He had no ticket, and the cashectomy required to buy one on the spot made that idea inoperable for the same reason there would be no sandwiches.

The employee's entrance he'd just been kicked out of was a no-go, too.

Toward the rear of the craft, though.

Lyn's gaze narrowed.

A low-ceilinged, broad gangway opened to a bay that was lit with harsh lighting that gave it a feeling of workaday austerity. It was a grimy, blocky, almost ugly cut in the station that had been cordoned off as much by its oily odor as by any particular attention to security.

The Service Bay.

Lyn's skin itched with anticipation.

He'd done repair work before. He could hum a few bars again.

The *Galactic Epic* was only a partial jumper, meaning it couldn't pull a full FTL—Faster Than Light speed. In fact, he was certain the Happy, Happy, Fun, Fun Cruise Lines didn't want it to because the two standard-week trek between the stars was perfect for bilking trapped tourists. *It's a locked house,* Lyn had explained when he lobbied James to take the audition. *By the time we get there, they'll be paying us to shut up!*

This meant it took huge amounts of raw material to supply each leg.

Time was running short. The crew, dressed in red, blue, and green jumpsuits and a variety of masks and breathers, was in full scurry mode, busting ass, and pushing big boxes of supplies and equipment this way and that.

He stepped forward, assessing the six or eight technicians he could see.

"Hey-ho!" Lyn said to a human tech as he drew near.

The tech was working at the front end of a rolling box labeled as *Fruity Nut Laser Boy Ice Cream,* pushing it over a rail and toward the hold.

"Day, mate," said the tech, puffing with exertion. "How are you?"

"I've been better, to be fair."

"Going to have to move away, sir," the tech at the back of the container said, this a mixed-race Blatipus, shorter than the usual Blatipus.

Rounder, too.

"Are you retaining water?" Lyn said before he could stop the words.

"Excuse me?"

The techs both grunted as they put their shoulders

to the task of keeping the container fully on the magnetic track it was supposed to be following.

"I was wondering if you might help a fellow out," Lyn said, ignoring the question.

"I said we need you to move," the Blatipus replied.

Lyn held his guitar up. "I'm the new singer. I just stepped out for a minute and now I've got to get back on before the gates shut down."

"Ah, yes. I heard we were taking one on," the human said. "Welcome aboard. More grist for the mill is more grist for the till I always say."

"Could I slip on in, then?"

"No can do, man. The Bay Leader will have our backsides if we let anyone sneak in. Just run down to the Employee Bay."

"Um … well … about that," Lyn hung his head, brain racing.

The human glanced at Lyn, then down to the Employee Bay where an androgynous half-human, half-something attendant glanced toward them. There was an expression on the attendant's face that was hard to decipher.

Lyn gave a coy smile and a gentle wave.

The attendant gave a tenuous wave back.

"Hmmm…" the tech said. "Girl problems?"

"You could say that," Lyn replied too quickly.

The attendant smiled at Lyn from the distance.

"If you get me in," Lyn said, lying. "I can get you tickets to the show."

"Like they'd let us go to a show," the Blatipus quipped.

Another container rolled into place.

Gates close in three minutes, the warning system reported.

Pops and squeaks came from the containers that were still being loaded.

"I can help get your job done," Lyn said, desperate.

"You're a bit artsy-fartsy for our kind of work," the Blatipus said, staring Lyn from head to toe.

"I'm desperate, man. What will it take?"

The human looked at the Blatipus. The Blatipus shrugged.

"How about an introduction?" the first tech said, glancing back at the attendant at the Employee Bay.

"An introduction? To her?"

The tech gave a wide-eyed expression of anticipation.

"The heart wants what the heart wants."

"I don't think that's your heart," the Blatipus said.

"Deal," Lyn said, figuring it could all work out. Somehow.

The human looked at the Blatipus.

The Blatipus gave a belch of a sigh. "All right. Go on in. But if you get caught it was the Deneb that let you in."

Lyn didn't have to be told twice.

CHAPTER 4

With the launch less than thirty minutes away, Lyn needed to move fast.

He slipped into a changing room and found a pile of discarded technicians' jumpsuits ready for cleaning. He grabbed the first one that almost fit and didn't reek of hard use. He ditched his duds, shoving them and Victoria into an empty locker.

"I'll be back for you, baby," he whispered lovingly to his guitar as he shut the door.

He'd get new clothes once he found James's assigned quarters—which, given his status as hallway grubber—would certainly be on the lowest of the lower decks. The grungier the better.

A check in the mirror and a flip of the hair proved that he could look like a tech.

Lyn slipped back to the busy service bay.

A door loomed in the back, obviously leading directly to the inner halls of the cruiser.

He needed to get to that door.

More important, he also needed to be able to move around freely until he could find James's digs.

A systems tech can go just about anywhere, though, as long as he looks the part.

He grabbed a device that scanned componentry, and then slipped a communicator into a slim pocket on the thigh of one leg.

"Look busy and you are busy," he said, quoting an old boss.

He grabbed a screwdriver, too. Just in case.

Just as he turned to the door, a loud call came across the Bay.

"Hey!" a hulking Rantari in a fresh-clean jumper yelled.

The fresh suit meant he was obviously the Alien in Charge.

He'd been talking to a tall, thin human dressed in an official-looking dark overcoat and a skullcap that matched.

Government man, Lyn assumed.

Checking up on the checking up.

Lyn took an immediate dislike of the man, but that was normal. Nobody likes a copper.

The Bay Leader stepped closer, clearly annoyed. He carried a glowing data stick and an ugly demeanor that seemed etched onto his deeply lined face. As he came forward, the Rantari pointed to a pair of huge crates waiting to get shoved from external point A to internal point B.

"Get to work—we got a container over there!"

"Will do, boss!" Lyn said.

He stepped toward the crates, but as soon as the

Rantari turned back to his data, Lyn made an about-face. A moment later he was through the door and standing in a dingy gray tunnel that smelled of oil and led right, left, and dead ahead.

He didn't know exactly where he was going, but down was down, and to his right, he saw a glowing outline of a lift tube.

"Well done!" he cried.

He couldn't wait to see the look on James's face.

CHAPTER 5

A firm voice echoed through the cruiser's nearly empty hallway.
Prepare for launch in five minutes.

Doors whisked shut, and the buzz of service drones scurrying to their launch positions filtered from the distance.

Lyn understood what that meant.

Five minutes until the auto-gravity system was turned off. He should have grabbed mag boots.

He clenched his teeth.

He hated zero-g.

Finding James shouldn't have been this hard, but the *Galactic Epic* was a big ship full of twists and turns, and passages that led to dead ends.

This is why the bastards inserted those guidance mind-maps he hated so much under your skin if you were a bona fide passenger. At least that's why they *said* they did it. Once the chips were installed, they logged into a person's brain stem and gave them the sense of place a person needed to navigate the corridors of the cruiser—zero-g or not. They also pumped you full of every metric ton of advertising they could cram in, and whatever BS propaganda the cruise lines wanted you to hear.

See the Sag A* Black Hole! Ride Rigel Falls! Experience Adventure on the Venusian Slopes!

Regardless, Lyn didn't have a chip.

Which meant that now he was as lost as a lawyer at a Conscience Conference.

He turned another corner. Nothing.

He was on the lowest deck. He was sure of that.

Pretty sure, anyway.

He'd gone down as far as the service tube could take him, and the only other passages down led to engine and power holds. The walls here were an ugly, sometimes water-stained, gray. The lighting was meager, and the halls smelled with an undertone of sweat and misuse. No paying customer would be submitted to this kind of abuse.

So, this is where the lowly help would be stashed.

And James was about as lowly as there could be.

A pre-launch light flashed red.

A clatter of heavy footsteps came from down a long hallway that jinked to the left.

A phalanx of security guards rounded the corner, a loose-limbed Tavarian and a pair of humans at the front, their skintight blue and red emergency suits stretching under muscles pumped up to make them look like superheroes.

"Hey!" a human at the front called, noting Lyn's presence. "You need to get back to Service Bay."

Lyn turned and ran, which, in retrospect was the wrong thing to do.

The guards immediately took to chasing him down, feet clopping in loud clangs due to the mag boots they wore to deal with possible zero-g work. Luckily, those boots slowed them down.

Still, they were in shape and just as fast as Lyn.

The clang of footsteps running his way drew closer.

If they caught him, they'd figure him out—eventually. Coppers were slow, but not totally dumb—and he always found their predilection to assume he was guilty was a pain in the ass, basically because he always was.

He took one turn, then another.

Alone for an instant, he paused at a doorway and slammed his hand against the locking mechanism.

Nothing happened.

Footsteps clattered nearer.

The hallway T-ed off ahead.

Left is best, he thought, unless it's right.

Heading left, he took another quick turn and found himself in a dead-end. A doorway to his left, and another to his right, but sealed shut ahead. The doors each were lined with locking screens built into the gray walls.

Heart racing, he grabbed the utility sensor he'd picked up at the Service Bay.

Lights flashed as it synched to the locking screens.

Footsteps paused at the T-shaped intersection. "That way," a voice rumbled. Footsteps clunked nearer.

He pressed a flashing blue button.

The door to the right slid open.

Without a second thought, he dashed in and toggled the sensor to shut the door behind him.

It closed with a near-silent thunk.

"Oh, thank the powers," he said, lifting his head and turning to put it back against the wall.

"Well, well," a low, feminine voice said. "Look who the quantum cat done drug in."

CHAPTER 6

Pressing his back to the wall, Lyn scanned a cramped little cabin to find two women.

Both young.

One dark complected with darker hair and a skin tone toward purple, reclining against a pillow in the tiny twin bed nearest him, its non-existent headboard pressed against the tiny room's barely painted side wall. This, Lyn realized, was the one who had just spoken. The other stood across the "far" distance, her head craning toward him after having obviously been interrupted while scanning the stars from what might well be the smallest porthole in the galaxy. Her skin was a shade somewhere between maroon and orange. Her white hair was cut short and parted on one side. Her eyes were a blistering blue.

Outside the hallway, footsteps from security clopped down the way, voices echoing.

"Oh, isn't this just too purrrrfect," the woman at the porthole said, leaning back against the cruiser's wall in a fluid motion that seemed familiar.

"Do I know you?" Lyn said, scanning them.

"I'm Doozie," the one on the bed replied in an obviously put-up, coquettish voice. She pulled one languid knee up as she came to a sitting position. Her toes seemed to bend upward in a stretch, then she rolled languidly to the side of the bed, her dark hair falling over the side of her face to reveal an almost elvish ear, pointed at the tip.

"And I'm Fae," said white hair.

Lyn's face dropped. His heart braced cold.

"The Feral sisters," he said, leaning his head back further against the wall. "Why'd it have to be the Feral sisters?"

Doozie stood up, so close to him now that her body heat was impossible to miss.

She ran the back of her hand softly down his cheek and jawline and came even closer.

The smell of something flowery came over him.

"It looks like our little contract jumper is in some trouble with the law, Fae-sie girl," she said, the corners of her lips turning upward in something Lyn hoped wasn't the silently deadly need for revenge.

"Maybe we should turn him in?" she continued, gaze hardening. The pressure of her body suddenly against his chest and hips wedged him defenselessly against the wall. "You know, tit for tat?"

"I'm sorry, girls," Lyn said, trying his best not to stammer. "I'm so happy to see you again."

"I'm sure you are, darling."

"Seriously. It's not like that."

"You mean it's *not* like you offered to join our act and then backed out at the end?"

In complete conflict with her suddenly constricted eyes, Doozie's voice was almost syrupy smooth.

"Well. Yes. That happened. But. No. Um. But…"

"That's a lot of buts," Fae said from beside her porthole.

"We can let bygones be bygones, right? I mean…"

Her lips seemed to get all pouty now, and with full pressure applied, Lyn's body began to betray him.

Lyn stifled a whimper, hearing voices outside the hallway again.

"Whaddya think, Fae?" Doozie asked her sister, though her gaze never left Lyn's. "Can we let bygones be bygones?"

"Well," Fae said. She stepped close enough that Lyn could see her now. "We could try him out again, I suppose. We never did find a guitar to fill the hole."

"I'm sorry, girls," Lyn said, his brain racing.

Doozie put her lips against his ear. "What's the matter, Guitar Boy?" she said. "Bite off a little more than you can chew?"

"Oh, I can chew with the best of them," Lyn replied. The footsteps outside had receded, and he was getting his bearings. At least he could remember their names now. Though, perhaps that had something to do with proximity. The cabin itself was considerably more than intimate, and he was pretty sure he was feeling the familiar presence of a tentacle wrapping around one knee.

"Big words," Doozie said.

"Believe me, the … um … chewing is fine. But I can't play with anyone at all right now, you see."

"Your fingers don't look broken to me," Fae replied.

"That's because they're not." He raised his hands to his shoulders, back against the wall, and waggled them, sheepishly.

Fae took one of his hands in hers. Her fingers seemed to flow over his, molding herself over his entire hand. "Still with the Middly-Piddly?" she asked.

"You mean the Intergalactic Band of Brilliance?" he replied.

"Whatever."

"Um. No," Lyn admitted. "Sadly, that is a thing of the future once again."

Fae shrugged.

"So…what gives, Guitar Boy?" Fae said, bending backward. "Why you say you no can play?"

"Well, it's more like if the cruise director sees me on this ship again, I'm getting dropped through the airlocks."

"I see," Doozie said. She turned to her sister. "Looks like we've got us a little stowaway."

"Tasty."

"So, we're going to need to work out another arrangement. Find something fun to do with him for a while."

The sisters shared a moment.

"I like how you're thinking," Fae finally replied.

"Another arrangement?" Lyn said.

Doozie looked down.

It was impossible to hide his interest in other arrangements.

"Well," Lyn said with a smile that was maybe a little out of control. "I've never been a kept man before."

"Don't get your hopes up too soon, human."

"What do you mean?"

Doozie's eyes went to steel. "We get you out of trouble now, you play with us after this gig is done."

"Um. That could be arranged."

"You do what we say. Scale for two months, starting today. We get an option to renew for another two months. Negotiations open after that."

"That seems a bit harsh."

"Well, I don't know. I understand getting dropped out of an airlock only hurts for a while. It's a free world. Make your choice."

"I seem to be a little out of options right now," Lyn said.

"We'll need you to sign a contract, of course," Doozie said, stepping back and sitting on the bed.

"That won't be a problem," Lyn said, beginning to unzip his service tech jumper.

"What are you doing?" Fae said.

"I'm … uh … preparing. I've always heard launch carousing is the best carousing."

"That won't be necessary right now, darling."

"But?" Lyn was stymied. "I thought…"

"Well, maybe sometime," Doozie said. "But we're on in five hours and us shapies need our reconstruction sleep."

"So, what do you want me to do?"

"We could use some extra towels," Fae said.

"Towels?"

"Tell the concierge that you're our new PA. Put the tip on the cruise lines."

She waved him out.

"Tut, tut."

"What about the entertainment director?"

"I would suggest you not let him see you."

"But...what about..."

"Tut, tut," Doozie said, curling into her bed. She waved a graceful hand in a dismissive flow. "Tut, tut."

Blinking back uncertainty, Lyn glanced to the door, then the sisters.

"What part of tut, tut did you not understand," Fae said, sliding into her own billet. "I suggest getting to it before we get to launch time. Zero-g with an armful of towels can be a real bitch."

Lyn shrugged. He wasn't sure how this day could get much worse, but he didn't want to tempt fate.

"Extra towels coming up."

He stepped to the door, then out to the hallway.

As the door slid shut behind him, another opened down the way.

A woman stepped out. Human this time—or at least Lyn was as certain of it as he could be anymore. She was slight, and also young. Thin dark hair in somewhat of a bob. She wore a loose-fitting shirt and dark scout pants suitable for traveling.

Seeing Lyn standing in his tech jumpsuit, screwdriver still in hand, she gave a relieved gasp.

"Oh, great! I need my shower fixed!"

"Yes," he replied. "How great it is. I've got no idea how to do that, though, ma'am."

A crestfallen expression came to her.

"Can you at least take a look? I hate to be dowsed on launch. Or, if you can't maybe you can just use your do-dad thing there to call over and get one of your little buddies down here? I tried earlier, but no one seems to care about this deck."

He grimaced. If he didn't try the system, she'd know he wasn't part of the service group. If he used the system, assuming he could work the device right, he'd give himself away.

At least now he knew how the day could get worse.

He raised the screwdriver as if it were a sword.

"I'll try, ma'am. Show me the shower."

CHAPTER 7

Despondent, James tumbled into his cabin. If you could call it that.

The place was barely a closet, crammed with a worn mattress and a rusted-water sink station built into the back wall. Good luck bending over in the "shower," which the administrator promised would once again be zero-g capable "soon."

A cloud of dust rose from the mattress as he fell on it, clutching his guitar close to his chest.

A rancid smell rose with the dust.

He barely pulled his feet in fast enough to miss getting his ankles crunched as the compression door slid shut behind him.

The sight of his fluffy shirtsleeves made embarrassed waves churn through his stomach. A sharp, metallic clamor of crewmates settling in came through the cabin's thin walls.

"Crap," he said to the walls. "How did this happen?"

But he knew exactly how this had happened.

Lyn, the walking, catastrophe had struck again.

He imagined his brother now, slinking away through Cygnus Station to get into who-knows-how-much-trouble. A cold shudder went down his spine. James knew better than to leave Lyn to his own devices. Whatever happened to Lyn now would be as much his fault as his brother's.

They *did* need the money, but there should have been another way.

Now what?

He'd signed the contract. It was a done deal.

A crushing sense of loss made it hard to breathe—or was that a reaction to the dust?

"I'm sorry, Mom," he said to the ceiling. "I got caught up in the moment."

Feeling morose, James Moore did what he did pretty much every time life handed him something he couldn't deal with—he grabbed his guitar, fiddled with the settings, and began to play whatever came to his head.

A minute later, or was it an hour later, a voice came from the intership communicators.

"The Cruise will launch in five minutes. Please enter full preparation positions."

He paused his playing and scanned the cabin.

No seats, he thought.

No restraints.

Crap.

Laying on the bed, he pressed his palms against the wall, and was happy when his feet could press against the opposite. The wonders of small cabins. He could hold the position for a bit, anyway. At least until the artificial gravity system could kick in.

Assuming, that was, this deck even had artificial gravity.

Grumbling, he stashed his guitar under the bed and laid back down, waiting and worrying, and wondering what horrible future news awaited him about Lyn after this cruise returned.

He hoped bail would be less than his paycheck.

CHAPTER 8

The "all clear" tone rang, indicating *Galactic Epic* had achieved deep vacuum, and that it was safe to move about.

James let go of the wall and was pleased to find artificial gravity was active.

He enjoyed zero-g well enough but found it to be more of a pain in the ass now that he was older. As directed, he went to the entertainment office down the hall and received his assignment: Second Six. Crab Nebula Bar and Bakery.

"Second Six?" he said.

A man dressed in the blue and black togs of The Grand Magician—a beloved character from an older Virtchie—was picking up his schedule, too. His face, checkerboarded gray and white on one side, was iconic. "Welcome aboard," he said, offering a hand. "Newbie human?"

"Totally," James admitted, feeling sheepish as he shook it.

TGM looked human enough himself, but there were

close fits around the galaxy, so the magician seemed to be one of them.

"The ship keeps a Galactic Standard twenty-six-hour clock. Thirteen hours in the morning, thirteen in the evening."

"And second-six is basically 1900 military," a young woman dressed as Princess Warrior Daphne added as she slid her time chip into the system. Her mop of wavy hair was augmented to forest green, with pink and orange streaks along respective temples, and the skintight military uniform which would be at least partially covered by a projection cape while she was on the floor showed all the proper curves.

The likeness was eerie. James wondered if her rounded eyes were real or had been augmented.

"It's a little weird, but you get used to it."

"Let me guess," James said. "That's the average sleep day of the average species around the known world."

"You've got the dart in the bull's eye, I'd say," replied The Grand Magician.

The Warrior Princess beamed an overly enlightened expression. "You have to wonder how many executive vice presidents it took GCL to make such a difficult and complex decision."

"And how long of a vacation they needed afterward," James said.

She laughed.

"Oooo, the stress," he added.

Both Magician and Princess took James in, glancing at each other.

"You'll make it here, I think," she said. "Sorry to hear about the time slot, though."

"Second-six?"

"I call it the Dead Zone. You go in but you're never sure you're getting out."

"Sounds … um … unpleasant."

"Early evening is a crap shoot," the Magician said. "Kids of every species coming down off sugar highs and parents ready to consider horrible things that probably should not be considered."

"It's Not. The. Best. Shift." Warrior Princess D said.

"The early hours everyone is happy-happy and the place is mostly quiet because the 'guests' are off doing hard rides and holo chambers. After Second Ten, the kids are all dropped into their sleep chambers, and you get nothing but older buggers wanting a moment to themselves. But yeah. Six to Ten." He shook his head.

"Dead Zone," Princess said again.

"Wonderful," James replied, though to be honest, he couldn't really imagine it was that bad.

At least he'd be playing music. And this was the Happiest Place in Space, right?

How bad could it be?

CHAPTER 9

The *Galactic Epic* had hit open vacuum five hours ago, and it had been like the hordes of Hell had been released.

Masses of families flowed up and down the corridors, from small parent-child groups all the way to the quail-like flock of Tuggari—a species that required four parents to mate, and created several dozen puffballs of kids that would eventually grow up to look like a construction crane had crashed into a praying mantis. Then there were the tours and the expeditions—the collective communities that had corralled every youngster possible and crammed them onto a vacation getaway.

And then there was the building, which James had no other word for but gaudy.

Galactic Epic's passages were huge and smoothly sculpted, the walls arcing up in a rounded bowl that was acoustically engineered to capture enough sound to ensure the horde of kids and toddlers didn't sound like a banshee's wail.

The whole thing felt like he was inside a huge, brightly lit pink clamshell.

Lights glittered.

Images flickered, and a character from every Happiest Place in Space VRVideo stood at every conceivable photo op stand.

All the while, the strains of *It's an Amazing Galaxy, Baby*, played on an endless loop.

James had been prepared for the idea that the entire ship was just one massive store, but to see it played out in front of him was something colossally breathtaking.

Guitar in hand, though, James picked his way through the crowded cruise deck to arrive at the Crab Nebula Bar and Bakery at exactly second-six o'clock.

Simply drawing near the Crab Neb was enough to say the shop had been designed to adroitly perform a cashiotomy on any family still standing after a long day at the cruiser's pre-arrival parks and holo-rooms—assuming the other stores and dispensaries hadn't completed the job, first. Then, of course, there was always debt to build.

The mixed aroma of liquor and sugar treats wafting freely from the Crab Neb combined to give the average passerby an immediate brain-freeze contact high, and the gentle breeze wafting from a set of gossamer-winged fairy fans in the ceiling tiles finished the deed.

"Fairy Fans," his data feed said when he noticed the blades shimmering with a prismatic sparkle in the ceiling lights. *"The very thing that completes any toddler's bedroom! Put them on your Galactic Cruise Line credit line and get free interstellar delivery!"*

As he neared the bar, James shut off the feed and scanned the floor.

Already the Crab Neb B&B was full of kids being sold sugar buns, and parents who needed to imbibe mood-altering elixirs to enact an immediate reduction in blood pressure.

Now it was his job to entertain those masses.

He leaned over the bar and extended his hand to the manager, a stocky Zubian—as if there was any other kind—who was standing behind the bar and fiddling with the control system responsible for the robots who did most of the work here.

Zubians were a species from a distant planet in the Beta Hydrae system. They were all stocky because they evolved in the weird gravity fields of a double star. The woman had a stern look about her, though, which he assumed was because the act of running a bakery and bar in the middle of the Happiest Place in Space was enough to turn anybody hard as a rock.

The strains of *It's an Amazing Galaxy, Baby*, were already clawing to get out of his eardrums, and he'd only been on Main Deck long enough to make it to his perch.

He couldn't imagine what it would be like to work here full-time.

"I'm James Moore," he said.

"Oh, wonderful," she replied, waving a disinfectant wand of UV over the glasses. "Perfect timing. You can call me Naomi."

"Interesting name for a Zubian," James replied.

"I would ask you to call me by my given name, but

you can't say it if you don't have a bone in your tongue."

"Naomi it is, then," James said.

"James Moore," the Zubian repeated his name, stretching her lips around the *James* as if it was a chore, then drawing out the *Moooooore* as if he were a cow. "Kind of boring, isn't it?"

He laughed. "It's better than Lyn."

Her three eyes gave an expression.

"Nothing," James said, waving away her unspoken question. "Inside joke."

The Crab Nebula Bar and Bakery was nestled in the middle of a spoke off the Main Deck's central hub.

It consisted of a central island in basic black, from wherein bartenders and baker robots delivered their products—the robots each coming complete with a design scheme meant to mimic a character. Despite himself, James's heart gave a cool little flip at the site of DX38, the Little Space Fighter. He'd always loved that guy.

A raised rail cordoned off the Crab Neb's floorspace from the main corridor.

A collection of heavy tables, adjustable memory foam lounge chairs, and isolation chambers sat at angles on the floor around the bar, and a huge pair of square, zero-g TARs (tumbler adventure rooms) were built into each end—each now crammed full of bouncy kids from six to twelve years old, or literally anyone whose parent or significant other was desperate enough to shove them into the container. The transparent walls showed kids zooming from handhold to handhold and perch to perch as if they were superheroes who had mainlined pure adrenaline.

Twenty clacks an hour, a sign beside the closest tumbler square read.

A deal at any price.

At least the tumbler rooms came with noise-reduction equipment. In a TAR, no one can hear you scream.

"Where do I set up?" he said.

"You'll play over there," Naomi said, indicating a platform nearby. "I hope you like children."

"I love children," James replied, "they go great with a little salt and cheese."

The proprietor laughed at him. "That's good. I like mine with tabasco and *grenich.*" Then she leaned into James's ear. "Just don't let the bosses hear you talk like that."

"Right-o," James said. He wasn't sure what *grenich* was, but he figured he'd look it up later. "Thanks for that."

"Eh," Naomi shrugged. "I do what I can. Now get to work or I fire your ass."

James chuckled as Naomi pointed to the stage and then turned to check on a server.

The "stage" was a raised platform floating on the artificial gravity system—meaning it hovered maybe half a meter off the ground. It glowed with some kind of piezoelectric shimmer, casting rainbows of color about as he stepped on it, and then kind of puddled out as he took his place on the round stool that lifted out when he arrived.

He took his place and settled in.

At least the guitar felt good under his arm and against his hip and thigh.

He'd brought the twelve-string with automatic key scaling but left the scaling turned off. Nothing annoyed him more than a player who needed a machine to put him in the right tune, thank you very much. Music was about people. Even the screw-ups.

He liked the look and feel of the twelve-string, and he decided to use it today because he could make a better sound with it. Playing in an open space, that seemed useful. At the time, anyway.

Now, among the clatter of the churning masses, he wasn't sure if anything mattered at all.

Glancing up, he saw a thin woman walking down the corridor.

She stood out because she was defenseless—walking alone rather than toting kids—and because she wore the simple black and white uniform that marked her as a server in the conservatory.

They locked eyes.

She was cute.

He gave a wry grin, which she returned with a coy shyness then she waved at him with a little waggle of her fingers.

He waved back, then glanced around the floor of the bar and bakery. It was maybe two-thirds full of kids and parents. Even then, conversation buzzed—mostly parents and kids mapping out every minute of their next two standard weeks.

He didn't want to see what it looked like packed.

When he looked up, she had walked past.

Sigh.

"Welcome to the *Galactic Epic*, and thanks so much for coming to hear me play," he said, noting the platform came with a remote mic system that broadcast his voice around the area. A few heads lifted his way, then went back to their doodles and games. "I hope you all have a great little vacay!"

A smattering of applause came, and two kids whooped.

"All right then," James said.

He strummed a G chord to check his tune, then fiddled with the high end until he had it right.

Then he dove into his acoustic version of *Happy, Happy Fun,* the tune he'd written with Lyn to support the *Galactic Epic* and this Happiest Place in Space tour.

Entertainment Director Dude was right to enjoy it, he thought.

It was a fun little song. Very snappy.

His fingers flew up and down the fretboard, feeling better as he settled in.

That was the thing about music for James. No matter what else was happening in the rest of the world, he always felt better while he was playing. There was something almost fractal about it, something fascinating in the juxtaposition of ultimate control and total chaos that playing brought him. The two essences clashed together inside his brain and just made everything feel…good.

Percussion came from the ball of his fist.

A lead ran from high to low, bending up while his thumb wrapped a bass line.

When he got to the spoken bit, he channeled his inner Lyn, which was fun.

He always admired his brother's ability to go outside the lines and just let things happen.

Then he was done, filling space with an extra "Happy, happy, fun" before blasting the ending chord.

The sound faded away into silence.

Or, rather, not silence—instead, the chord faded into the rumble of families still talking about plans and a mother complaining that neither of her kids was eating the cake she'd just spent a week's wages to buy them.

On the stage, James clamped his jaw tight.

It was going to be a long two weeks.

CHAPTER 10

Nearing second-ten o'clock, James thought perhaps he might just rather die than finish.

He'd played theme music to what had to be a billion movies—then a medley of all of them together, then the same set list again at the "requests" of every whiny kid of every whiny species on the ship, including one that had no actual mouth to whine with, but managed to nonetheless.

The aroma may never leave James's shirt.

Three rounds of *Happy Family Fun* with toddlers break dancing on the carpet made him simply hate that song now.

So, as he came to the end of his set—or was it his sentence—James decided to drop one piece in just for himself. Just one.

The piece he'd begun to pick out in his cabin pre-flight came to him.

His fingers took the position.

As he played, words came to him as if from nowhere.

Just a stanza, but it was the right stanza.

A stanza that said there was more here than he'd found.

> *You've got problems*
> *You've got torn wings*
> *Sometimes it feels like*
> *You've lost everything*

He loved it when writing came that way. Like a gift from the center of the world.

He slid his fingers up the frets, looking for space and creating ideas on the spot.

"What are you doing James Moooooore?" A voice crashed into his party.

It was Naomi.

He stopped.

"We're not paying you to do that crap. I want Galactic Cruise Lines music. Not self-pretentious syrup you dredged out of the airlock."

"Sorry," he said.

As if on cue, the next act came to the floor, carrying a box that looked like a cross between an accordion and a blowfish.

Glancing at his internal clock, he realized it was time.

Thank The gods.

He was so happy he didn't even ask about the instrument. Just grabbed his guitar and moved toward an opening in the rail. If he moved fast enough, he could be out of sight in less than a minute.

Something grabbed his arm.

"Wow," a voice beside him said. "I can't believe you're so multi-talented."

When he stopped to focus, he saw it was the woman from earlier. She'd changed from her server's uniform, and now wore a comfortable green and blue shift that came to her thigh and exposed her shoulders and a touch of collarbone.

"Thanks," James said.

"I don't care what that lady behind the bar said, I loved that last piece best."

He smiled wider despite himself. She seemed excited to see him.

"It's hard to believe you can fix showers and play as well as that, too. I should probably have guessed it from your fingers. They seem so ... long."

The expression on her face was somehow intimate in a way that made him uncomfortable.

"What are you talking about?"

"I'm giving you a compliment, silly. Not many service techs can say they're real musicians?"

"Seriously, miss," James said. "I have no idea—"

He stopped.

Service Techs. She said service techs. When he and Lyn had last split, Lyn had found grunge work doing repairs and maintenance.

"You're telling me," James said. "That I fixed your shower?"

"Among *other* things," she replied, smiling with an

obviously put-upon wicked sense of innocence, her eyes shining in the gossamer fairy light.

"Lyn," he said as if to himself.

"Don't be silly," she said, putting a thin hand on his shoulder. "Of course, I remember your name!"

James felt a blush raise to his cheeks.

"Well," he said, calculating quickly as they stood there in the middle of an aisle. He wanted to keep her talking. Wanted to figure out how this whole thing with Lyn had come about. "I'd love to hear more about you. How about a drink?"

"Oh, you mean like a real date?" The woman fanned herself with one hand.

"Of course," he said, gesturing to a pair of semi-isolated seats at the edge of the Crab Nebula Bar and Bakery's reach. "Just like."

A moment later, they were seated.

A robot server took their order.

"So," James said. "Tell me everything."

CHAPTER 11

If Lyn was going to keep James from going ballistic supernova in the most public of ways, he was going to need to get out and about. And if he was going to get out and about *without being noticed*, Goal One had to include getting rid of this idiotic service tech jumpsuit.

If nothing else, it was getting more rancid as time went.

His presence would be memorable for all the wrong reasons.

He also wanted to retrieve Victoria. Just the idea of the poor little thing being all by herself in that cold, dark locker room was giving him hives.

"We don't want Guitar Protective Services to come down on us, now, do we?" he said to himself as he lay sprawled across both twin beds, which was the only way he fit in the compartment from head to toe. "That would be bad." The mattresses were an annoying combination of soft and lumpy that he wasn't sure he'd ever be able to sleep in, even though he was tired and a little sore from the evening's "activities" with the showerhead woman, but now was not the time for sleep.

With the cruise now officially launched, the sisters were finally out playing a show. And with the lower decks quieted down due to their underpaid and overworked inhabitants mostly being out on their assignment, Lyn wouldn't get a better chance.

Now or never, he thought as he slipped away from the sisters' room.

It was good luck that the timing was between shift transitions, meaning the Service Bay's locker room should be empty.

He arrived to find the bay filled with the low buzz of routine operations.

Automatic conveyor systems sorted containers of material into their proper positions. Robotic muscle moved boxes from point A to point Z. Lights flashed and buzzers buzzed. Everyone seemed content. The place even smelled like it was under control.

Lyn hated it at first sight.

Pools of overseers stationed at regular intervals observed operations, several focused on scanning the mechanicals. Their faces were set in those bored but satisfied frowns that seemed to scream *I can't wait for this goddammed shift to be over*.

Overseeing mechanicals was dumb, Lyn thought, but someone had to do it.

He put on a nonchalant "I should be here" air and made his way to the locker room. The service bay was probably the only place on the whole of the *Galactic Epic*

THE HAPPIEST PLACE IN SPACE!

where the technician's uniform helped him stay in the shadows.

The trip was easy.

He slipped into the dingy locker room to find his stage costume was still in the empty locker he'd left it in, as was Victoria. Of course, if there was an outfit less inclined to let him fade into the crowd than the service uniform, it would have to be this fluorescent lemon-yellow stage costume.

Life as a personal assistant, aka groupie, to the Feral Sisters was turning out to be a steady stream of one disaster after the other.

He'd have to borrow something.

Scanning the area for options, Lyn noted that the locker system consisted of three rows of cubbies, each secured with biometric locks. Of the unassigned lockers, only the one he had commandeered held anything.

The showers and zero-g lavatories wouldn't serve any purpose to him now.

A new pile of soiled jumpers waiting for the laundry run was no better.

He pressed his thumb onto the pad of one of the locked cubbies and received a red flash and a *go away you farking idiot* message.

"Grand," he said, anger rising.

He ran his thumb across them all, just to get the whole string flashing at once.

What the hell, right?

You only live once.

Toward the back, the controller's office peeked out, a glass wall separating it from the main locker area. A narrow, poorly lit hallway led from it to the lockers. The light coming from it made Lyn take an involuntary half-step back.

Something caught his eye.

His heart leaped.

There.

In the corner of the office was a rack and on the rack was a dark jacket and multi-toned blue, teal, and purple hat that was an interesting mix of bowler and Stetson.

The office was empty. The controller elsewhere.

Perhaps that was him in the meeting room across the way from the office, where he could hear voices but not make out words.

Cautiously, he edged closer.

The voices grew louder, but he focused on the office and its rack of clothes.

Yes.

Total payday!

Folded on a chair beside the rack. Pants and a shirt to go with the jacket and hat.

The controller apparently changed his own duds in the "privacy" of his office and assumed his position was enough to keep the riffraff from taking what wasn't there. Luckily, he hadn't counted on the riffraff being Lyn Moore!

Lyn hunched down and, keeping his head under the profile of the office wall until he got to where the doorway stood open, duckwalked as cool as any Chuck Berry impersonator had ever duckwalked.

As he did so, a cat, gray and male, stepped quietly out of the office where the conversation was happening.

Lyn almost toppled in surprise.

It was smallish for an obviously grown tom, but

bulky. Muscular, not fat. Short Maltese hair, and green/yellow eyes that focused on him like the cat couldn't tell if Lyn was a threat or simply dinner for twelve.

Surprised, Lyn stopped in his tracks.

The voices grew louder, and he motioned the kitty to stay quiet.

Yes, he felt stupid the minute he did so.

The cat's expression grew bored, but kept its intense gaze directly on him, holding a countenance that said he was still deciding if he would rather take a nap or gouge a piece of Lyn's shin.

What the hell?

Was it the service controller's cat? An employee's? Just another stowaway?

He didn't know, but the last thing Lyn needed was to have a feline intruder give him away now.

The cat sat upright, pulled up a forepaw, and—extending one talon—began to clean (*or was that sharpen?*) that talon with a harsh motion that, as far as Lyn was concerned, felt like a threat.

One false step, that talon said, *you get this right across the face.*

It was enough that Lyn felt certain muscles tightening in ways that were more than uncomfortable.

The cat let Lyn enter the office, though.

Lyn took one more look at the cat, and decided he was in too far to back out now.

Rolling from duck walk position to crawling on all fours, Lyn shuffled to the chair, picking up the shirt and pants and cradling them in one arm.

There were shoes, too, but they were too big—something that made Lyn wonder about the other clothes, but he figured he could make do with too large there. He was no beggar and chooser.

The shoes were ugly, too. He'd rather go barefoot. So ixnay on the oozeshay.

The jacket, though.

That, he liked.

He could see wearing it on stage, really. Soft and something toward synthetic snakeskin. Just looking at it made his fingers ache to play. It would catch the light in that perfect way that good stage clothes had.

Finally relaxing, Lyn could make out the conversation.

It was definitely coming from the small office across the way.

"I told you, Crawford. It just doesn't work that way. We can't be digging into the bins every time you get a tickle up your ass."

Lyn gave a wicked and sad smile at the same time. Logistics. You wouldn't find him caught dead in a logistics job.

"I don't care what you said, Jayal," Crawford replied in a controlled tone. *"We've got a prospective buyer on the hook. So, I need the crystals and I need them now. I know neither one of us want any accidents to happen now, do we?"*

Lyn frowned.

He'd been on the back end of that kind of tone before—complete with a quiet edge that conveyed so much more than whatever words were included in the message. Crawford sounded miffed. And Crawford sounded like he wasn't taking 'no' for an answer.

The word 'crystals' stayed caught in Lyn's ears.

Whatever was going on, it most definitely was not some random conversation about a standard shipment.

Crawford was some kind of muscle.

After a long hesitation, the first voice responded.

"I'll need some time."

"Much better, my friend. I think you're making your way back to our good side. You've got until tomorrow, second four."

There was a long pause.

"All right."

Suddenly growing anxious, Lyn pulled the jacket down off the rack, and for good measure, the hat, too, then, slapped the hat onto his head and—as quietly as he could while cradling shirt, pants, and jacket, and giving the cat a silent nod of thanks—crawled back to the doorway, turned into the hall, and stepped calmly back to where he could duck behind rows of lockers.

Just in time, too.

As he caught his breath, the two speakers emerged from the meeting room.

Whipping the hat off his head, Lyn peered out from the side of the row of lockers to give a little peek.

One was obviously the controller.

The other …

Lyn frowned hard, clutching the clothes tight to his chest and turning back to hide.

What the hell? he thought again, realizing it was rapidly becoming his go-to phrase.

Crawford was the government guy he'd seen in the Service Bay when he'd first become a stowaway. The overseer of the overseers. Lyn would recognize him anywhere. The man was a walking cliché. Still tall, still thin. A human scarecrow still dressed in that official-looking dark overcoat, which was now thrown over his shoulder, and a skullcap that matched. His shirt was dark, too, going with his pants. His Adam's apple bobbed as he swallowed.

What would a government man be doing twisting the bay controller's arm for access to whatever these crystals were?

The obvious answer struck him.

Crawford was no government guy.

Crawford was a crook.

The door to the locker room whisked open and Crawford went to it, then paused.

"Come along, Frisky," he called.

The cat stood up and sauntered after the crook, giving Lyn a sideways glance as he passed the row of lockers.

I allow you to live another day, the glance said.

Nothing else came of it.

The door slid shut.

The sound of footsteps came, then the sound of a heavy weight falling into a chair told Lyn that the controller had returned to his office. The man pounded his fist on something Lyn assumed was his desk.

A beep from the communications system later, the man asked for "Stubby" to join him.

Realizing time was short, and that he didn't want to be there when Stubby got here, Lyn spun on his heel, grabbed the hat again, and made for the door.

It slid open as he approached.

A moment later, he made his way back to the public hallway.

• • •

Lyn found a restroom, grabbed a stall, and did a quick change.

The pants were too big, but he could cinch those up. And, yes, the jacket was sublime. Its excess material gave him a frumpy but modern-day dashing look that he knew would play well enough. In fact, the jacket might be too much. He didn't want to catch eyes.

The shirt, though…

It was an off-white T-shirt that almost fit. Lyn shouldered it on, pulled it down and straightened it. Yes, it was large, but then he looked at it.

"Space Dancer," the stencil read in blue and pink. A gold flare came from the active thread array it had woven into it.

What an eyesore.

Well.

Thank the powers for the jacket.

And the hat, for that matter. He pulled it over his forehead and dipped his chin, suddenly feeling very much like a spy. "Duh-duh-duh!!!" he said, taking a pose.

From nearby came a nasally laugh. "What the hell was that?"

Lyn saw a man had stepped into the room. Embarrassed, he just went with it. "I'm Inspector Holmes," he said. "You know, from the vidsie *The Sleeping Beauty of Baskervilles*. Surely you're not on a Happiest Place in Space cruise without knowing one of the franchise's greatest characters?"

"Hmpf," the man peered at him.

Lyn ducked under the brim of the hat a bit.

"Dumb shirt," the man said, exposing himself as an asshole.

Lyn shrugged. The last thing he needed was to get caught up in a tiff with an idiot. "I think the fellows who designed it are laughing all the way to the cash machine," he said, then stepped out.

The sisters would expect him in the room soon, but reputation was on the line.

James would be "playing" the Crab Nebula.

He headed that way, avoiding security systems by ducking behind kids and parents and big, bulbous images of characters. An aromatic train of sugary ghost fairies slid past. He blinked away a scintillating display of dancing teapots.

As he went, he realized something had been wiggling its way through his thoughts the whole time he was changing clothes.

The crook, Crawford, was talking about crystals.

Crooks didn't talk about things that weren't worth anything—and a crystal sounded like it would be worth a bunch.

How much?

Lyn had no idea, but he'd guess it would be enough to afford more than a couple sessions in a studio. If he could manage to grab even just one, that would mean James could blow this gig off, and they could record again.

As twins, they had always been two planets orbiting a single asteroid, right?

He liked that.

Simple and efficient.

By the time Lyn stepped into the corridor, he had set a new course.

He needed to find this Crawford guy, and maybe pay him a visit.

He put his hand in the jacket pocket and ran his fingers over the technician's scanner that was the only thing he'd kept from his time as a service worker. It would come in handy if he could find the right door.

You've got until tomorrow, second four.

Crawford's words kept going through his head.

Yes, he thought as he slipped with some degree of incognito into the Main Deck.

First, he would save James from total embarrassment, then he would make them rich.

Just the thought made his fingers itch to play.

If the maps were correct, the Crab Nebula was just ahead.

Time to go to work.

CHAPTER 12

James had a Kantorian Mule, and the young woman a cosmic pink Mai Tai.

The seat was cushy enough that he would have considered coming here to catch a nap if it wasn't for the masses of people streaming past, the blowfish accordion music his follow-on act played, or the strains of *Amazing Galaxy* that filled the space around them.

By whatever random powers served the world, James hit paydirt right away.

"Well," the woman said as she sipped her drink. "My name is short for Cicely. It's what I called myself when I was little," she explained, smiling pleasantly. "Cissy. My Granny thought it was cute, so she called me that forever. Now, every time I hear someone say it, I think of her."

James gave her a response that seemed delighted enough, and she continued to talk, filling in one of those canned versions of her life story that everyone carries around with them. He was certain it would have been interesting.

His mind was too preoccupied, though.

All he could picture was Lyn, and all he could think about was that he was on board.

And that James needed to find him before the authorities did, because only those same random powers could say exactly what kind of trouble his brother could get in if left to his own devices too long.

Fifteen minutes and another Mai Tai later, James thought he had the whole thing between them figured out.

Cissy was a first-time cruise worker. She was assigned an equally dingy cabin as James, in the same deck as James, but in a different wing. Lyn had stumbled upon her and … well … he'd been wearing a service tech get-up, and she had a shower to unclog.

The rest he could imagine without being told.

"And what cabin number would that be, again?"

She told him, winking, "as if you don't know," she said.

Yes. He knew how to get there.

James gave it some thought, it made sense Lyn would find someone to mooch off and the only people either gullible enough or kind enough to help him out would be other entertainers or cruise workers. He'd give even odds that Lyn was holed up down in the worker's deck right now. The only question was why he'd stowed away.

Of course, with Lyn, looking for reasons was farcical.

"Do ya wanna go back there now?" Cissy said, raising an eyebrow.

James sipped his drink to create a moment.

Cissy was certainly attractive. More cute than stunning, which was definitely his type. And she'd been fun to talk to.

But he felt queasy with the whole thing.

He and Lyn had played that twin game before, and, sure, the hijinks around it could be fun. But the stakes were high now, and he didn't have the bandwidth for this kind of stress. He couldn't tell her what was going on without putting both him and Lyn in potentially hot water. He couldn't reveal that despite having rooted out her shower, Lyn was most definitely *not* a service tech, and he certainly couldn't let her know that James was most definitely not Lyn.

If he clued Cissy in, she'd likely—and justifiably—get pissed off. And if she got pissed off enough, she'd let the Happiest Constables in Space know there was a problem.

Beyond that, he simply liked her too much at this point.

The idea of playing a game on her felt bad.

He checked his internal data feed.

"I would love to do a reprise," he replied, flashing her a Lyn-like grin. "But I need to stop by the entertainment director's office in fifteen minutes."

"Later, then? Afterward?"

"Wouldn't miss it," he replied.

"When you come by, can you wear your technician's suit again," she said, running her Mai Tai swizzle over her lower lip. "That was kind of fun."

"My, my," James replied, putting his drink down. "What would your Granny say?"

"Granny was a dancer for the Raging Comets when

she was my age, so I figure she'd be giving me pointers."

"Touché." He laughed. "I think I would like Granny."

"You got a thing for older ladies?"

"Um … that's not exactly what I meant."

She laughed at him.

"Bring your guitar, too," she said, her eyes getting dreamy. "I really did like that piece you were playing. Is there more?"

"I'm sure there is," he said. "I'm just not sure what it is."

"Maybe we can pull it out of you."

"We?"

"Me and Granny."

"I see."

And he did see. She was definitely his type. Sassy and quick-witted, and not one to take any crap.

"Well," James said, standing. "I have to be going. Places to be, you know?"

And rooms to search, he thought. *Brothers to read the farking riot act to.*

"How long will it take?"

"To be fair, I don't know," he said, being both honest and diversionary.

"Well … don't be too long."

He tipped a fake hat. On the outside he smiled, but on the inside he groaned.

Goddammit, Lyn. Why'd you have to go and screw this one up?

He looked up then, and his chest clenched.

Despite the jacket and the stupid hat, he would recognize that stride anywhere.

Lyn.

Making his way down the corridor toward the Crab Nebula.

He glanced at Cissy, then at Lyn in the distance.

His brother caught his glance and froze.

Thank God.

"Um ... I'll see you soon," James said, then, gripping his guitar, rushed away.

"Tell the entertainment director I said you need a raise," she said as he left.

CHAPTER 13

James caught up to his brother at the entrance to the Orion Belt Battle virtchy experience, just as three interestingly garbed teens were stepping out—line tape over various strategic locations on their bodies, and holographic skin replacement creating the pebbly essence of the Belladon species, who were from Bellatrix but were aggressive enough that they were one of the few inhabitants of the galaxy that decent people still didn't accept in their ranks. War sabers and plasma propellants slung low dangled from belts looped around their thin waists. They were still high from the battle, still *pew, pewing* each other as they turned down the corridor and toward the gift shop.

James avoided them and stepped boldly forward to block his brother's progress.

For just an instant he considered smashing Lyn with his perfectly good guitar.

"I see you've met Cissy," Lyn said with a cheesy grin.

"What in Hell's name are you doing here?" James

said. He grabbed his brother by the elbow and pulled him along the corridor behind him, doing his best to not make a scene by running.

Lyn scurried, holding the hat to his head.

"Hey, watch it with the jacket, man!"

"You idiot," James said. "You're going to get us both tossed out the airlock."

Lyn yanked his arm from James's grasp and the two came to a halt amid the stream of cruisegoers. He peered over the throng, ducking his head down under the hat brim again. "Cool down, man. We'll only hit the airlock if you keep making everything so farking obvious."

"Crap," James said, turning his body to hide his brother from most angles. He stared at him, full truth settling. "I can't believe … how did you get here?"

"It's okay. You don't have to thank me."

"Thank you?"

"You knew I wasn't going to let you ruin our good name, didn't you?"

"What?"

"What do you mean, *what?*"

"I don't have time for this, Lyn."

"You know what I mean, brother. We really can't be busking now, can we? We'll never live it down."

"Busking?"

"Busking."

"Busking is fine. A lot of great people got started—oh, crap, man. See what you've got me doing? We need to get you out of here. If anything is going to ruin our reputation, it'll be you getting shown the brig for stowing away on a galactic cruise liner."

"Don't bet your home asteroid on that," Lyn said.

"I'm betting."

"Getting nabbed for stowing away would be so much cooler than what you're doing."

"I'm doing nothing but playing music."

"See what I mean? You're already calling that hellacious lounge crap 'music.'" Lyn gave the air quotes.

"Shut up."

"Next we'll be playing the Vacation Inn there in the nether regions of some broken down belt in the *Where Are They Now* system."

"I'm serious, brother," James said. "Shut the hell up or I'm just going to turn you in myself."

"At least people will sleep well."

"And what's with the dumbass shirt?"

Lyn glanced at his chest. The "Space Dancer" lettering flared purple.

"You can wear it if you ask nicely."

"I swear I'm going to hit you over the head with another shoe if you don't can it."

"I'll sic Mom on you if you do."

James did a doubletake.

"I've done it before," Lyn added.

"She'll be on my side," James finally replied.

"No, she won't. I'm the youngest."

"By three minutes."

"Besides, I'm here to save you."

"Save me?" James said. "You? Save me? You've got to be kidding me. The only thing you're doing here is rooting out shower drains." He glanced back toward the corridor that led to where he assumed Cissy was still at the Crab Nebula. "Among other things."

Lyn gave a cheesy, tooth-filled grin.

The shoe bit was an old family joke, but it was better to rely on the tried and true than to punch his brother out on the spot.

"You can't fool me, brother," Lyn said. "You know you hate doing that gig as much as I hate imagining it."

James drew a big breath, then paused.

Around them, families floated by. The strains of *Amazing Galaxy* seeped back in, and James felt his stomach twist.

"See?" Lyn said. "I'm right. You'd rather suck down a Fangorian Hot Toddy than play another gig at the Crab Neb."

James hated it when his brother was right. "It's not the most fun thing ever."

"There's a silver lining for you here, right?"

"You mean the cash."

"I mean with me being here!"

"Then, no. I most definitely do not see any silver lining."

"I can take some of your gigs!"

James chuffed. "I can think of no way in which that is a good thing."

"Of course you can. I take your gigs and that leaves you free to sit in that piddly little cabin and whine about being shackled with a more brilliant and better-looking brother! Win-win."

James stared bullets.

"All right. Never mind that. I take your gigs, and you cloister up and write your songs, or whatever the hell else you want to do."

"While you save our reputation?"

"Exactly."

"You're insane."

James opened his mouth to reply further, but then thoughts came.

The idea wasn't horrible, really. At least, now that Lyn was actually on the ship, there was nothing to do but try to keep him from exposing them. If one of them were always in the cabin it would at least ensure no one would think twice about both twins being on board.

"With two of us stuffed in there, the cabin will get pretty stuffy at night," James said.

"Um," Lyn replied. "That really won't be a problem."

"Go on," James said, Lyn's tone already sending a tingle of worry dancing on his spine.

"Go on where?"

"Don't be stupid. Just the tone of your voice is making me queasy. Your crappy little grin is simply adding to it."

"I've got … um … commitments elsewhere."

James's face fell. "Cissy." He hadn't realized how much he'd enjoyed talking to Cissy until this moment. "You're staying with her?"

"No. Not exactly Cissy."

"Where are you going to be, then, if not our cabin?"

"Um … well …"

James waited. Then he caught on.

"The Feral Sisters?"

Their name on the bill caught his eye earlier, bringing back memories of the night he and Lyn had first met them. It had been in a dive on Luna. Lyn had almost been roped into playing a sideman contract gig for them, but they'd gotten out of it on what was essentially a technicality and a wave of popularity based on a quickly improvised gig.

That had been a great night.

The pained expression on Lyn's face said it all, though. James's brother had gotten tangled up with the sisters.

Again.

"How?" James said.

"It's a bit of a long story."

"*Now* you're getting closed lips?"

"Let's just say I have a new contract to play out." Lyn shrugged.

"You actually signed a contract this time?"

"Well … it's not like I had any real choice. And it's not really that bad."

"You're doing anything they say, right? How can it not be bad?"

Lyn seemed to shrink for a moment. Then he drew a breath. "Well … there are some side benefits."

"Side benefits?"

Lyn gave a nonchalant shrug.

"Oh, crap," James said.

"They're very *bendy*."

James grimaced. "What am I going to do with you?"

"You're going to give me your gig tomorrow, that's what. I'll come by your place to pick up your guitar about half past second five?"

"My guitar?"

"Won't look right if I'm up there with Victoria now, would it?"

James nodded. "I see that."

"And your duds, too."

James started to argue, then took another look at the "Space Dancer" shirt, which was now flaring magenta and yellow.

The idea would actually solve a couple of problems. If Lyn was indebted to the sisters, they would keep him out of the corridors, and as long as he didn't screw up too bad he could probably play the Crab Nebula well enough. If they could manage to keep it up for two weeks, they'd be free.

"All right," he said. "Let's try it. I'll see you then."

CHAPTER 14

Lyn took his seat at the Crab Nebula, cradling James's guitar and running his fingers over the strings in preparation. He liked the sound of the twelve-string. He should probably play it more often.

But Vicky. Well, she could be a jealous guitar.

He'd exchanged clothes with James, too, and as far as anyone was concerned, that's exactly who he was. As if anyone cared. He'd kept the jacket, though. He'd been totally right about its great stage presence. The thing gave off a perfect vibe. Understated, but obvious.

Better, though, the pockets were as big as everything else.

And in this case, the jacket pocket was big enough to hold the system tech's synching device—something he expected he'd put into use after the gig.

Everything was going according to plan.

At first, he'd considered telling James about the crooks but then realized what a gargantuan mistake that would be. James was a brilliant musician, and a grade-A brother when things came to the pinch, but his ability to deal with risk—and the anxieties that risk caused—was best measured on the quantum particle scale. It would be far easier to simply grab a crystal from the bad guys, cash it out someplace, and make James a business proposition when the time came.

He'd already scouted three jewelry shops on the ship.

Or, if they wouldn't go for it, there was always Cygnus Station. The place was crawling with free market entrepreneurs willing to do any deal.

He couldn't wait to see James's face when he showed his brother a bona fide way out of their financial woes.

Just the thought of getting his hands on a crystal made his brain sizzle.

Gossip was good on the workers' deck, and it turned out that knowing your brother was too worried to stick his neck out of his cabin gave Lyn a certain amount of confidence…call it freedom, to poke his head in places he might be so inclined to poke.

He'd discovered Crawford's cabin number when a service coordinator complained that one of her bots had been turned off.

"The guy's a farking scarecrow," the woman said as she hit a jumpdust stick.

Her eyes had grown more glazed with the combination of dust and drink. A few comments later, Lyn confirmed everything. Room number, directions to it, and an idea of the service schedule the woman had programmed.

With just a little more luck, his system synch pad—

which he'd slipped into his jacket before going to James's quarters to make the exchange, would get him in later tonight.

Now that second four had passed, Crawford would be in possession of the crystals.

The challenge was to find a time when the crook would be gone from his quarters—a challenge Lyn had met by sending Crawford a complimentary ticket to the Feral isters' show this evening.

So, Lyn figured tonight was that right time.

Until then, though, he had a gig to play.

Having warmed his fingers up, Lyn glanced around the "room" to see the already hollowed-out expressions of families on day two of this cruise, expressions that said one of two things: that either this was truly The Happiest Place in Space, or that they would prefer a pulsar dog come along and eat their arms off to get them out of this trap. The trip had another three days of cruising on the flight plan before hitting the "real" park, and then another five days back. If these parents thought it was bad now, the best was yet to come.

Lyn grasped the guitar and strummed the entry to *Happy Family Fun.*

Time to pour some oil on the flame.

He planned to play that song over and over again, adding a different Moore brother flair each time. He assumed no one would even notice, and if by the randomest of chances someone *did* manage to notice, and if that somebody then decided to go to the viral public with it, well, that would be good, right? If his thumbing the nose at the Happiest Place in Space was recorded and broadcast across the galaxy, so much better. He knew their following. There's no such thing as bad press, after all. Tweaking his thumb at the Galactic Cruise Lines conglomerate with a forty-five-minute version of *Happy Family Fun* would be worth gold at the box office of public opinion.

At least in a certain sector.

So, he flexed his fingers, and scanned the families once again.

Gave his little introduction.

And broke into song.

CHAPTER 15

It was maybe a half hour into Lyn's rendition of "Happy Family Fun" that Cissy showed up, taking a seat at the front row table, stage left. For a working-class passenger, she looked good tonight, wearing a pair of dark maroon leggings under a sheer golden top that billowed about her and shimmered with photon flakes, and flowed to mid-thigh. A darker halter lay under the top. Her nails were painted black. Her short hair was pulled back with a metallic band that seemed to snap with minute bits of laser flare. Her skin was smooth. Her eyes were dark and glittering.

Lyn winked at her.

She winked back. Or maybe it was better to say she grimaced back.

He wasn't sure.

But she sat down and ordered a drink, then tapped her booted foot along with the tune.

For a few minutes, anyway.

Eventually, she grew bored, then realized what he was doing, and began to look around at the audience, complete with an expression that said "what the hell is this guy, doing?" only to realize that literally nobody in the entire area was paying any attention at all.

She turned her attention back to Lyn then, and a different expression came over her face. This one more amused. Contemplative. More enlightened.

It was an expression that included one corner of Cissy's lip curling up in a wry grin that carried an aura of off-hand respect as if to say *well done, cowboy.*

She raised her glass, and sipped, waiting for him to finish.

Fifteen minutes later, he did.

A smattering of something that might have been applause came as the guitar finally faded to silence.

"Play your song from yesterday!" Cissy called out.

Lyn smiled. "Maybe next set, Love," he said. "I'm off on a five-minute break, now."

Lyn put his guitar down and stepped off the platform to join Cissy.

"Well, that takes some *chutzpah*," she said. "A one-song set?"

"Just wait until they hear part two." He sat back. *"Happy Family Fun (reprise!)."*

She laughed. "That's almost worth staying just to watch."

Lyn raised an eyebrow. "Screw 'em if they can't take a joke."

"Is that what you said as you weren't showing up last night?"

"I didn't?" Lyn stopped himself, realizing almost too late that he was missing some information.

"Don't pretend with me," she said. "If you don't

actually want to meet up at a girl's place, it's always better to tell her flat-out rather than lead her on."

She sipped her drink and stared unflinchingly at him.

Suddenly, Lyn felt like he was working without a net.

Dammit, James, he thought.

Protocol for these things was always to tell the other brother what had happened so that they didn't get caught out.

She laughed at his expression.

"It's all right," she said. "Play my song first up and I'll consider giving you a break."

"I'd like a break."

"We'll see how well you play it." She took another sip of her drink, then waved a robot down to order another.

"Um…," Lyn said. "Just what song is that?"

"You know what song I want to hear," Cissy replied, lightening up further, and running a piece of fruit from the swizzle stick across her bottom lip. "The song I loved so much. The one *my Granny* was going to help write?"

"Your Granny? What does she have to do with—"

Lyn felt the pit open beneath him. That had been the wrong thing to say.

He knew it because Cissy's temperature dropped to liquid nitrogen in about as long as it took to put his foot in his overly big mouth.

Her gaze sharpened. Her lips compressed. He could feel smoke rising.

"Who are you?" she said.

Her eyes seemed to bore holes into his head. She crossed her arms, and sat back, appraising.

"Enough of a break, Guitar Boy!" a voice called from the Nebula Crab's counter as the robot delivered Cissy's second drink.

Naomi.

The manager calling him out.

At least James had been kind enough to let him know that much when he'd stopped to grab the guitar.

"Get back on the seat!"

"Duty calls," Lyn said, standing. "Got to run."

A minute later, he broke into another forty-five-minute run of *Happy Family Fun.*

When he looked back to the seat Cissy had occupied, it was empty.

CHAPTER 16

The good thing about Cissy leaving the Bar and Bakery in such a huff was that it meant Lyn was free to follow up on his plan to check out Crawford's cabin without making up something else that might get him into even more trouble.

Carting James's guitar case with him, he went first to the Feral Sisters show to poke his head into the theatre.

Yes, Crawford was there. Entranced, it seems.

Lyn supposed that's what happened when you tell a person that a shapeshifter wants to meet them. He hadn't been lying when he told James they were quite bendy.

Wasting no more time, Lyn went straight to the lift tube and piled in, clutching the guitar case to his chest.

When the door shut behind him, the tube was crammed with a critical mass of snotty-nosed kids and dreadfully droll parents that smelled of…well… smelled of.

Theme music was piped into the enclosed space,

saccharine enough that Lyn envisioned the use of a lift tube for solitary confinement. A person locked into this Hell would eventually go crazy enough to agree with or confess to just about anything.

As it was, one lift and he was already thinking he might fall to his knees bawling.

He couldn't imagine the pain if one were trapped here in an emergency.

Lyn's mind was preoccupied now, though. So, he made it through the ordeal without killing anyone.

Which was good.

Crawford's cabin number glowed in his memory. He focused to recall the passages he would take once he got to Executive Deck, which was where the crook was cabined. That meant it was important Lyn look like he belonged—and that meant he had to know where he was going. With the guitar case, he figured he'd need to look like an actual star rather than the lounge lizard act that James was. Another reason he was the right guy for the job.

While James would have been meek, Lyn could pull that off in a hard vacuum.

Artificial gravity grew more pronounced as the lift tube climbed.

Families peeled off at each stop.

By the time the lift tube came to Executive Deck, there was only himself and one other passenger. A three-legged pod creature with a set of snakelike heads that made Lyn think of Medusa.

"Business good this trip?" Lyn asked in the moment of silence they shared.

"Ssssso far, soooooo good," the creature replied with one head.

Its tongue flickered green. One hand on a flexible trunk of an arm patted a back pocket.

The lift halted at the proper deck.

A gentle tone buzzed, and the doorway slid open.

Medusa waddled out and turned left, which made Lyn happy.

He stepped right, swinging the guitar gently as he went. Artificial gravity made the case feel different here than it would on a "normal planet." Something about the attraction of matter inside molecules and certain electric or magnetic fields, or *some* other such thing that Lyn would never really understand—even though someone once tried to teach it to him at repair tech school.

Fancy that.

Regardless, the case swung like a normal case through most of its arc, but there was a hitch at the place it was closest to the floor, and where the shift from downward arc to upward arc made it pull a touch harder.

Most of the time that shift didn't even faze him, but *here* ...

Walking alone, down the long corridor of the executive deck...

Senses piqued...

Hair raising at the base of his neck...

Hoping to avoid problems as his gaze scanned cabin numbers...

Here, every little detail seemed ripe with meaning.

He felt the world around him suddenly as fragile as

THE HAPPIEST PLACE IN SPACE!

the crystal caverns of Sirius Seven, and even the extra weight of the case pulling against his hand drew his attention.

Crawford's room loomed.

With his opposite hand, he reached into the large jacket pocket to extract the synching scanner he'd taken from the Service Bay.

He stopped at the door and pressed a few buttons.

Lights flared.

Lyn waited for the telltale tones of a lock releasing.

Nothing happened.

Nothing except the hum of a hover cart arriving that grew louder as the cart turned a corner and headed his way down the corridor.

The smell of fresh fruit and warm bread wafted from the cart, obviously holding someone's dinner covered with a shank of white cloth. The service robot accompanying the cart was tall and slender, a figure Lyn recognized as a replica of Gandar the Thinman Tinman, a character in the latest Happiest Place in Space production. Lyn admitted he'd always liked Gandar. The robot had a sarcastic nature that made its storylines come alive.

"Can I help you, sir?" the robot said.

"Um," Lyn replied.

"Is your scanner broken?" the robot added.

"Yes," Lyn replied, keeping his cool. "Damned thing worked earlier today. But nothing's synching now."

"Let me be of service," the robot said.

A mechanical arm emerged from its skin. A light flashed green, and the door to Crawford's room opened.

Inside, the lights adjusted from dim to brighter.

"Thank you," Lyn said, tipping his hat.

"Please rate my service twenty-eight stars if you would," the robot said. "I would like to avoid being melted down."

"Twenty-eight stars it is!" Lyn replied.

He stepped into the room before the robot could refresh its registers and, as the door shut, Lyn gave an appreciative whistle.

Crawford was flying in style.

The chamber was so open and so broad that the rounded walls seemed to almost disappear into the distance. An equally round sofa was embedded in a sunken pit that appeared to have a zero-g field built under it. "Perfect for taking an afternoon float," Lyn whispered out loud. *Or,* he thought, *having a space dalliance anytime.*

A projector broadcast an image of their flight path through the galaxy, and a readout indicated the time left until their destination was made.

The aroma was fresh and simple. Clean, with almost a citrus flavor.

Synthetic statues filled three corners, their shapes morphing slowly into constantly changing figures. One was now something close to a famous work of a naked guy Lyn had seen before, but couldn't name. Another was a likeness of two guys on Vengartan horses, beating the shit out of each other with flailing clubs. He'd call that one El Ka-bong if it was up to him.

The third was of a kid getting his feet washed.

He admitted he'd never understood that kind of art.

It all seemed so Weenie Boy to him.

But more power to them, he supposed. Fandom wants what fandom wants, and to deride a person's fandom was both shitty and bad for business.

The whole thing—including the rounded, oblong kitchen island and fully-stocked dispenser bar built alongside it—made Lyn reassess his view of Crawford. One suspected that any cabin that an intergalactic crook would be stashed away in would be off-limits to a grunt. At least off limits to a grunt without an in.

Lyn had figured Crawford as a grunt.

But these digs said he was a bigwig.

The quickening in his chest told him he didn't want to know much more.

A short hallway opened behind the kitchen counter —leading obviously to the sleeping quarters. That's where anything he was looking for would be.

His boots softly clomped on the composite flooring at the entrance, then went quiet as he made his way onto the softer fabric flooring farther into the room. As he stepped past the kitchen counter, his ears caught another sound coming from the sleeping quarters. Water, maybe? The shower?

He paused.

Yes. Water was running in the distance.

"Hiiiisssssssss!"

It wasn't water this time. From the kitchen floor, a gray flash caught his eye.

The cat.

It launched itself at him, crashing into Lyn's leg with a heavy impact, and clinging onto his knee.

"Ahhhhrggg!" Lyn grunted.

"Hiiissssssssssssss," the cat called again as it swung

from his knee like a trapeze artist in a stellar vortex. Then it let go, landed, and stepped precisely away even as Lyn was still in the process of grabbing the wall, and then the counter, to keep himself from faceplanting into the kitchen island.

Along the way, he dropped the guitar case.

It landed hard, giving a discordant thump.

"What's that?" a voice called from the shower.

Panicking, Lyn took in the cat, who was now sitting calmly against one wall, staring innocently at Lyn with its eyes flaring golden flashes.

It licked its chops, remained silent, and created an essence about itself that carried the universal cat language of a bored shrug.

Asshole.

"Crawford?" The voice again. Thick and masculine. Definitely coming from the shower. "Is that you?"

Lyn stooped, picked up his guitar … er, James's guitar … realizing that—while the fabric of his pants was partially shredded—the cat had not actually scratched or clawed anything enough to break the skin.

Without time to question things further, he scanned the area for a place to hide.

The main door out seemed suddenly very far away, and to be honest, he wasn't sure he could get it open anyway. One problem at a time, though.

Instead, his gaze caught the corner of an open closet space.

A couple of steps and he could be there.

It was all he needed to see.

Picking up the case, and clutching it against his

chest, Lyn slipped through the bed quarters and stepped into the darkest corner of the closet.

Once he was sure he was hidden well enough, he slid the doorway just that much farther closed, quite happy he was wearing James's despondently dark clothes now rather than the flashing "Space Dancer" shirt he'd traded in.

He'd grown to kind of like that shirt.

Outside the closet, the water in the zero-g shower had definitely turned off.

Footsteps rumbled heavily on the floor.

"Is that you, you goddamned cat?"

From the angle he was at, Lyn watched the cat stroll into the bedroom quarters as the large man stepped naked from the shower. *Frisky*, Lyn thought, remembering the name Crawford had given it. He added one and one, and after doing some advanced-level calculus, realized Frisky was Crawford's cat, not this guy's.

Suddenly a few more things made sense.

Bigwigs or not, these two were a team, this guy and Crawford.

Crawford was the brains, this guy the muscle.

"Goddamned cat," the man said, making like he was going to kick the animal as he lumbered toward the closet.

Lyn understood what was going to happen.

The man was going to open the door, and Lyn was going to be exposed to the brawny part of the Space Mob Team, or whoever these guys were.

In that instant, Lyn laid out an entire fiction of intergalactic mob activity and found that every single thread wound up with him being hogtied and fed to the coldest regions of deep space. His stomach rose to block his windpipe, and for an instant, he was certain he was going to projectile vomit all over the guy as he opened the door.

In a flash, though, the cat leaped.

Yowling. Literally flying through the air with ears pinned back, claws flashing, and teeth barred, the muscular feline went directly for the beefy mob muscle's most tender nether regions.

The man's blood-curdling scream followed.

If he hadn't been petrified, Lyn may well have broken out in a fit of snickering laughter, but instead, he simply sucked in a quick breath and felt his own nether regions contract as the man crumpled to the ground. The floor shook under Lyn's feet as mob mass made a crash landing.

A river of profanity followed as the man cupped himself, groaning and crying as he rolled to his side.

The cat, collected once again, sauntered to stand patient guard beside the closet door and, once again, hunched down and began cleaning its paw.

Frisky glanced at Lyn, flexing a claw.

Lyn had never felt closer to an animal at any time before.

A song fell into his head then. A gift song, one of those things that only came around by the random happenstance of the powers that be, filling his head, fully formed.

With the man still crumpled, in a flash, Lyn heard it all race through him:

THE HAPPIEST PLACE IN SPACE!

I don't like the way, you treat my cat,
You'd better get out of here you dirty rat.
I'm sorry he scratched you, on the ball,
But you shouldn't run naked, down the hall.

Frisky my kitty, hurt my buddy, Frisky.
Frisky my kitty, hurt my buddy, Frisky.

My cat's not nasty, he's really nice,
Except maybe for, a couple of mice.
Well he might have a temper, and get out of line.
But truth be told, he's a damned fine feline!

Frisky my kitty, hurt my buddy, Frisky.
Frisky my kitty, hurt my buddy, Frisky.

I'm sorry.
So sorry.
He scratched you.
He really shouldn't have done that.
He's not very nice.
But what can I say?
He's Frisky, my kit-ay!

Ouch!

The song made Lyn happy, and despite the situation he found himself in, he very nearly broke out with a victory *huzzah!*

As he gathered his senses, the man's rumbly voice broke the song's spell.

"Crawford or no Crawford, I'm going to kill you someday," the man grumbled as he rolled to a sitting position, angled such that Lyn saw entirely too much.

The room grew deadly quiet.

Then.

From Lyn's jacket pocket, the synching device suddenly gave a soft vibration that said it was connecting to something.

Green light flared from it.

Lyn pressed a hand over it to hide that light, but another light—this one on the closet wall—flashed crimson in the darkness.

Beside him, a cold safe locker clicked.

A compartment in the wall ratcheted open.

There, with his eyes adjusted to the darkness, Lyn saw a long, low gem case.

Inside, he realized, would be the crystals.

His gaze went back to the man who was now standing before the door, and before Lyn.

"What do we have here?" he said as he peered into the corner of the closet.

Frisky gave a low growl.

"Shut up," the man said, kicking the cat aside and standing taller. His muscles flexed. "Looks like we have a little visitor, don't it?"

CHAPTER 17

Time stopped.

As he cowered, trying to auger himself further into the closet, Lyn's heartbeat filled his ears, and his breathing slowed to nothing.

The big, naked man standing before him flexed his fists, preparing to try them out around Lyn's neck.

The guitar case felt hard against Lyn's chest as he clutched it closer.

They were going to die together, he and this little twelve-string.

He considered hitting the man with it, but James was already going to kill him if anything had been damaged earlier in its crashing against the floor. Assuming he lived through this, Lyn would be able to adjust any tune that had been busted, but he had no idea if the first crash had broken anything, and using the guitar as an actual, real live weapon would not be good for the instrument.

Instead, Lyn reached down toward the wall and, as the man pushed open the closet door, wrapped his fingers around the edge of the crystal case. Scrabbling fingertips around the edges, he lifted it up and brought it crashing against the side of the crook's head.

The impact was sharp and solid. Wood against bone.

The man gave a sound that was something between a groan and a scream. A rush of air pushed through his lungs.

Oof.

Then he crumpled like a dead sack.

A wild bleating of sound filled the cabin then.

A security beacon of some sort.

The light on the closet wall flashed an even more intense red.

Holding the crystal case, Lyn looked left, then right, then down.

What had happened?

He looked at the drawer that had extended from the safe. Probably some kind of proximity warning. Who knew, though?

He stood there, frozen and cradling the guitar case in one arm and holding the case of crystals in the other until the cat's raw-throated meow broke his trance. The cat was standing now, staring out toward the living quarters.

"You're right," Lyn said to the cat. "Let's get out of here!"

Adjusting his hold on the guitar case, Lyn raced to the door, the cat sauntering behind at a pace more fitting the feline.

He put the guitar down, and pulled out his service tech device, praying it would work this time.

Lights flashed.

Nothing again.

A sound came from the bed quarters. The mob muscle, stirring.

Lyn's eyes grew wide, and he toggled the system again.

Still, nothing.

The cat, clearly bothered by something Lyn interpreted as a lack of patience, came closer, hunched down, then in a single leap landed on Lyn's shoulders.

"Ow!" Lyn said. "What the hell are you doing?"

The cat was heavy, but once again its claws didn't pierce skin. Its breath smelled of fish.

As Lyn stared, the cat simply batted a paw against a touch screen on the wall.

The door slid open.

Lyn blinked, then turned his gaze up to look at the cat, suddenly not caring about breathly odors.

"Good kitty!" he said.

"Come back here!" the naked man called from the doorway.

But, with both guitar case and crystals in hand, Lyn was already gone.

CHAPTER 18

When all seems hopeless
You trip and fall
The mountain looks tall
But it's a small universe after all

Sometimes I feel like screaming
Screaming out to the empty vortex
I'll close my eyes and start dancing
Dancing to better days ahead

Over the sound of his ear-clip system, pounding came to the door.

James thought *Galactic Epic*'s sound system was the one good thing on the whole package. He'd been able to record multiple tracks, which had really helped him dig deeper into the song. *It's a Small Universe, After All*, was growing to become one of his favorites.

THE HAPPIEST PLACE IN SPACE!

Once he realized what the pounding was, though, James jerked in response and yanked the ear clip away.

His track stopped, but the rest of the tune kept playing.

The transition was more than a bit jarring.

Turning the clip off, he looked up.

Only then did he begin to panic.

"Open the door, Moore!" a vaguely familiar voice came from opposite the wall. "We know you're in there."

He sat bolt upright. The pounding sounded official. He didn't realize he'd been making so much noise.

"Just a minute," he said, awkwardly struggling to untangle his crossed legs, put his guitar aside (actually it was Victoria, Lyn's guitar), and stand up. His legs burned with the tingle of having been crossed and bent over for too long in the tiny little cabin—a sign of how long he'd been working, and just how dialed in he'd been.

He made it to the door, though.

"So sorry to bother anyone," he said as it slid open. "I didn't realize I was making any disturbance."

By the time he was finished, the door had swiped its way fully open, and James realized this wasn't a noise complaint.

Three people stood there.

First, a burly Kadossian security officer, probably the *Galactic Epic*'s commander based on the sharpness by which he wore his gray pull-over sweater with epaulettes over long blue sleeves, collar turned down. All six of the Kadossian's eyes, and something that was almost certainly a plasma weapon, were focused intently on James.

Second, the portly entertainment director, cheeks even more brightly red with exertion than James remembered from audition day, and eyes dark and sharp with accusation and anger.

And third, Cissy, hanging in the back, peering around the Kadossian security officer, gaze glaring.

"What?" James said, his brain crashing thoughts against each other.

"See, Inspector?" Cissy said. "I told you. He's dressed totally different."

James glanced down at his chest to see the gaudy "Space Dancer" lettering flash in its light fantastic splendor.

"Lyn," he said before he could stop himself. Realizing there was nothing to be done to cover things up, James felt his shoulders slump as the air went out of him. "What's he done this time?"

"Gig's up, kid," the entertainment director said. "Tell me where your brother is, or this will be the last time either one of you ever plays again."

James stammered.

"I got nothing," he admitted as he felt the truth fall over him. It was past time of the Crab Nebula gig, and Lyn hadn't returned to retrieve Vickie. "He could literally be anywhere."

At that moment, the lift tube down the corridor opened, and Lyn came tumbling out, guitar case in one hand, a box of dark wood in the other—a gray cat holding onto his shoulder for dear life, but somehow looking good doing it.

THE HAPPIEST PLACE IN SPACE!

"What the—" James said.

Seeing the reception party waiting for him, Lyn came to a screeching halt.

The cat gave a deep *merrowww*.

For a moment it looked like Lyn might bolt.

"Wait!" James called, realizing the game truly *was* up. "Come here, Lyn," he said.

His brother appeared to see the game was up, too. He stood taller and shook himself off as if he was trying to add back whatever dignity he might be able to find. For an instant, James wondered if that wasn't the cat rubbing off on him.

Except, of course, that ability to put on airs of dignity, come what may, had always been a thing about Lyn.

Which, come to think of it, was very catlike.

"Inspector!" Lyn said to the Kadossian as he came forward. "Just the man I was looking for." He proffered the wooden case. "I think you'll find the contents of this quite interesting."

A sharp beep came from the inspector's communicator.

The inspector answered the call.

"What is it?" he said with no little aggravation after toggling the system on. "I see." He waited. "Yes. That's right. I'll be right there."

The officer looked at the entertainment director. "I need to go."

"You can't go now," the director replied. "You need to arrest these kids. They need to be locked down."

"I'm sorry, Irvin," the security leader said. "There's

been a disturbance on Executive Deck. You know what that means."

"We've got an obvious stow-away situation," the director argued. "How much bigger of a crime can you get?"

The inspector shrugged. "Company directive," he said. "Sorry."

The cruise director seemed to deflate.

"Executive Deck?" James said. His stomach was tingling. He didn't like how that sounded.

"Um, I might be able to shed some light on the disturbance, Inspector," Lyn said.

"Of course, you can," James groaned.

"Some light?"

Lyn pushed the case at the inspector again. "It's a long story, but I think you've got some crooks on board."

The inspector took the case, flipped it around to face him, and hit the fasteners.

The lid levered open.

Inside, the gleaming light of a thousand metallic stars flowed outward, covering the raised ridges of the Kadossian's features with golden highlights and dark crevasses.

He looked back at Lyn, then to James, eyes glittering.

"I need both of you to come with me," he said.

He snapped the case shut.

CHAPTER 19

It was four hours later.

The inspector had already arrested both Crawford and the naked guy.

The entire case of what had been stolen gemstones from the 43 Antarean Dynasties were in *Galactic Epic*'s evidence vault, and rumors that more arrests could be coming were circulating around the entertainment crew. The inspector was playing that part close to the chest, though—or close to whatever Kadossians considered a chest.

Lyn and James—and the cruise director—were in the Chief Security Inspector's office.

Cissy had given her story and been let go.

Given that Lyn and Frisky appeared to be something akin to inseparable now, the burly little cat was here, too, curled up in a ball and presumably sleeping, though James had his doubts.

He kind of liked the cat, but he wasn't certain.

The thing seemed like a natural-born killer.

He'd keep his eyes peeled for a while.

"You're telling me," the inspector said to Lyn. "That you slipped back onto *Galactic Epic* to investigate this intergalactic crime ring thing yourself?"

"Well, I didn't know it was an intergalactic crime ring when I did it," Lyn replied. "I realize that what I did might not seem the wisest thing," he added, glancing at the entertainment director—who was clearly unhappy with this turn of events that might result in the brothers getting some form of leniency. "But I stumbled on the possibility that the crystals were on board by accident, then I couldn't let it go. The director there had just rejected me, and, as my mother would say, there wasn't any time to dilly-dally around. So, I snuck back through the Service Bay and began to poke around."

James fought the urge to raise an eyebrow.

Knowing his brother, there was likely at least a respectable piece of the truth embedded in this story, just like there was always a piece of truth in pretty much every story they would tell their parents growing up. *Plausibility is valuable,* Lyn would say as they'd plot their talking points. James found himself wanting to know what parts of his brother's story were true and which were twisted, but there would be time for that later.

He'd had enough of questioning and depositions.

Right now, he just wanted to get out of this room.

"I see." The inspector frowned from his ridged brow. "And your interaction with Miss Taylor?"

"Miss Taylor?"

"Cissy," James said. "Jesus, Lyn, you really need to focus on people."

Lyn gave a wide-lipped expression that was half grin, half grimace.

"She asked me to fix her shower, so I did."

"She's a very nice girl, Inspector," James said. "I'm certain she didn't have anything to do with anything here, other than to get tangled up with my brother and me. We'll do our best to make amends."

The director broke in, pointing firmly at Lyn. "Enough of all this. The young man clearly stowed away. That's a spaceboard offense that's subject to some pretty extreme fines. I want you to lock them up."

"Well, Irvin," the inspector said. "I can do that, but I'm thinking it's going to look pretty bad for at least one of us if I do."

"How so?"

"I understand that the Galactic Cruise Lines front office has already learned of the daring deeds of these brothers. They're advertising them as headliners, I think. *Come cruise with GCL and join heroes like the Moore Brothers* and all that crap. So, I suspect that means they're going to have a sizeable offer heading their way after they leave this office."

There was a moment of silence.

"I see."

"So, if I were you," the inspector said, "rather than pushing to get them thrown in the brig, I'd be working to get them a prime slot on another cruise." Three of the Kadossian's eyes blinked. "It's your call, though. How much do you like your job? I can certainly hold them if you press charges. But in all seriousness, they've just brought down a huge piece of the Space Mob. I don't think you're going to win here, Irvin."

The director sat back, pulled his jumpdust stick from behind his ear, and stared up at the ceiling as if asking the gods for forbearance.

"Um," Lyn said.

All eyes turned his way.

"There's one more thing, too."

"What?" the director said.

"I've got this little contractual thing going with the Feral Sisters that I might need you to buy out."

The entertainment director gave Lyn the side-eye, chuffed, then glared at the inspector.

"I hate you," he said.

CHAPTER 20

"Well," Lyn said as the brothers walked through the captain's corridors to take a lift tube back to their new quarters, the cat strolling along beside them. "That went about as well as it could have."

"You have a strange definition of *well*, brother."

The passages here were businesslike in that sterile way office space always has. Laid out in squares. Filled with a mass of people and drones, though James wasn't certain which were more mechanical. The more he was in these spaces, the more James knew they weren't cut for him.

"We've got a gig, anyway," Lyn said. "A real one, you know? Not like the crappy Crab Nebula."

"That part is good. I guess the Dude understood the better part of valor, anyway," James said.

For the first time ever, the idea of playing a cruise made him happy.

For the rest of the trip, the brothers had an early slot on the main stage. And they got a better bunk, too. Bigger anyway. Still down in the dungeons of the workers' quarters, but big enough they could stretch a little. They still needed to hold the slot down at the Crab Neb—at least until they docked at Aldebaran park and the director could acquire another act. But that was only for a few days.

And their next cruise gig would be even better.

Full-bore headliner.

"A veterinarians' cruise!" Lyn said. "How cool is that?"

Frisky looked up, gave a deep grumble, then hissed.

"Can't possibly be more annoying than the Happiest Place in Space," James said. "It'll pay well, too."

"Exactly," Lyn replied. "Though that's kind of secondary now, isn't it?"

"The money is why …" James stopped.

The expression on Lyn's face sent a chill down his spine.

"What is it?"

Lyn reached into his pocket and pulled out a single crystal. It was dark, translucent indigo split with writhing elements that glowed with golden warmth.

"Oh, Lyn."

"It was too pretty to pass up."

"You know we're going to have to leave that here," James said.

Lyn sighed.

"Yeah. I know."

They came to the door of their new cabin. It slid open to reveal a space that wasn't much, but at least beat the single slab of a place James had been in. Their guitars and James's wardrobe had been moved while they finished helping the inspector tie up loose ends. A few more cruise line branded garments had been delivered for Lyn.

The cat entered first, then gave a meow of acceptance.

"What's with him?" James said.

Lyn smiled. "I think he decided to adopt me."

"That's a cat for you."

They stepped into the room.

It didn't stink like James's first cabin.

"What do you want to do until our next show?" Lyn said, stretching out over one of the beds.

"I don't know. I need to talk to Cissy sometime, though. If nothing else we need to apologize."

"Yeah," Lyn said. "I didn't know it was going to turn shitty like that."

James nodded but kept his mouth shut. Lyn was good at heart but blind in the head. Most everything he did turned out in ways he didn't know in advance.

"What about you?" James said. "Now that you're legit, what do you want to do?"

"I'm thinking we go down and enter the *Mr. Epic* contest."

James laughed, stretching out on the other bed. Outside the port hole, stars of deep space gleamed. "Nothing like dancing around in front of a whole boatload of worn-down parents."

"We'd win in a landslide, don't you think?" Lyn said.

"Well," James said, contemplating. "If we didn't, at least we'd know the game was rigged."

"Totally," Lyn said, sitting up. "Hey. Speaking of Cissy, teach me that song of yours."

"Which song is that?"

"The one she was asking me to play at the Neb. I don't know what it was, but the way she talked about it, it sounds really good."

James nodded, smiling and swinging his legs over the edge of the bed.

He hoped she'd forgive them.

"All right," he said, picking up his guitar. "It wasn't really done until just a little bit ago. Or rather, just as they were pounding on the door—so she hasn't heard the whole thing."

"That's cool," Lyn said. "I like being the first to hear what you do."

James strummed a chord, grimacing at the guitar's sound.

"What the hell happened to this?"

Lyn shrugged.

James adjusted the tune.

When he was ready, Lyn leaned in.

And James began to play.

CHAPTER 21

You've got problems
You've got torn wings
Sometimes it feels like
You've lost everything

When all seems hopeless
You trip and fall
The mountain looks tall
But It's a small universe after all

Sometimes I feel like screaming
Screaming out to the planet Zorb
I'll close my eyes and start dreaming
Dreaming of better days ahead

You're overwhelmed
And people need you
Airlocks and robots
won't fix themselves

When all seems hopeless
You trip and fall
The mountain looks tall
But it's a small universe after all

Sometimes I feel like screaming
Screaming out to the empty vortex
I'll close my eyes and start dancing
Dancing to better days ahead

You've lost a lover
You don't feel good
You'd fix that sector
If only you could

When all seems hopeless
You trip and fall
The mountain looks tall
But it's a small universe after all

Sometimes I feel like screaming
Screaming out to the planet Zorb
I'll close my eyes and start dreaming
Dreaming of better days ahead

I wish I was 5 foot 10, but I'm 5 foot 1
I wish I spoke Zubian, but I can't speak the tongue
I wish for money honey, but I have my health
I wish for health, but I don't have money honey

I wish for glory, but I remain ordinary
I wish for fame, but I'm stuck on this ship thing

THE HAPPIEST PLACE IN SPACE!

I wish my brother would behave, but man can he sing
I wish things were different, but I love my life

I love my life,
I love my life,
I love my life,
I love my life.

YOU'VE REACHED THE END!

We hope you've enjoyed the raucous cruise through the galaxy! If you have, you might find other books in the series to be equally as fun.

Also, if you enjoyed this book, your review on the book retailer of your choice is a great way to help us out. Even a quick line or two can help!

Thank you so much for reading our work!

ACKNOWLEDGMENTS

We would like to thank all the people who have helped us make it this far in life—but, man, that would be a nearly infinite list. Instead, let's narrow it a little. Thanks to all the sets of Collins brothers who came before us. Thanks to Dad, especially, for hanging around while we were brainstorming a bit.

Thanks, too, to Kristine Kathryn Rush, Dean Wesley Smith, and Lisa Silverthorne for throwing their own ideas at us when we asked for a bit of advice. That was a fun lunch.

Thanks to our beta readers, Sharon Bass and John Bodin. You two are the bestest.

Thanks, also, to Karen and Lisa for not laughing at us when we decided to take a flier at this silliness—with special focus on Lisa for being our last reader!

And, finally, thanks to the many airplanes that flew over our recording studio as we were grabbing the audio version of this book. Or, um, actually, no thanks there. Those planes were a real pain.

ABOUT RON & JEFF COLLINS

Jeff and Ron Collins—the original Cruise Brothers—first played music together as youthful teens down in the basement of their home in Louisville, Kentucky. *("No grass, but a lotta grapes!"* - inside Mom joke, there*)*. While occasionally annoying the family and their beloved cat Frisky with boisterous songs at 2am, there were some gems that have managed to stand the test of time (a few even found their way into this Cruise Brothers series).

Then Jeff fiddled around with theater and improv comedy before hightailing it out to Los Angeles to become a rock star, and Ron found his way through engineering and into the life of a high-powered icon in the science fiction field.

Or something like that.

Now here they are. Back, better than ever.

Aside from composing and producing original works, these days you can find Jeff playing live with several tribute bands, including a tribute to Genesis (Gabble Ratchet), Alice Cooper (Pretties For You), and Jane's Addiction (Jane's Addicted).

Ron's short fiction has received a Writers of the Future prize and a CompuServe HOMer Award. His short story "The White Game" was nominated for the Short Mystery Fiction Society's 2016 Derringer Award.

With his daughter, Brigid, he edited the anthology *Face the Strange*.

You can follow Ron at his website: Typosphere.com
Or join Ron's Readers and get two free books!
typosphere.com/newsletter/

ALSO BY RON COLLINS

Novels

Stealing the Sun (9 books)

Saga of the God-Touched Mage (8 books)

Fairies & Fastballs w/Brigid Collins (3 books)

The PEBA Diaries (2 books)

The Knight Deception

Wakers

Collections

Holiday Hope

They Came Back

Collins Creek (Vol 1) Contemporary Currents and Historical Eddies

Collins Creek (Vol 2) Streams of Speculation

Collins Creek (Vol 3) Tides of Adventure

Tomorrow in All the Worlds

Picasso's Cat & Other Stories

Five Magics

Novella

The Bridge to Fae Realm

Poetry

Five Seven Five (100 SF Haiku)